An Unlikely Gift

Acknowledgements

Thank you to the following people for reading, critiquing, and editing this story. It's a better book because of you: Julie Cosgrove, Linda Daniels, Jo Huddleston, and Amber Tinsley.

An Unlikely Gift

by

Vickie Phelps

Copyright © 2022 by Vickie Phelps

All rights reserved.
No part of this publication may be reproduced, distributed, or transmitted in any form or by any means, including photocopying, recording, or other electronic or mechanical methods, without the prior written permission of the publisher, except as permitted by U.S. copyright law.

The story, all names, characters, and incidents portrayed in this production are fictitious. No identification with actual persons (living or deceased), places, buildings, and products is intended or should be inferred.

Cover Design: Judie Korbelik

ISBN: 979-83637-8065-3

"*Every good gift and every perfect gift is from above* ... "
James 1:17

Chapter 1

Cara Phillips unlocked her car door and slid into the driver's seat, What a day! Sam Perkins had worked everyone at the law office to the bone for the past three days so he could spend his Thanksgiving holiday on a cruise. "I'd like to put a hook in him and reel him in just so I could throw him back over the rail of that cruise ship to the sharks," she muttered to herself as she put the key into the ignition. "Making Olivia and Emma cry with his criticism and condescending words." She let out a deep sigh. Sure, Mr. Perkins had been under stress, they all had, but did he have to take it out on them?

She backed out of her parking space and onto the street. She couldn't wait to get home, kick off her shoes, and put her feet up, but first her stomach demanded a stop at Ralph's Grab It 'N Go to pick up some of his delicious spicy barbecue. Tomorrow was Thanksgiving Day, and her mom would have a wonderful meal for the family, but tonight, she wanted something she didn't have to cook.

She pulled into the parking lot and frowned. Ralph had gone all out decorating the outside of his store for the holidays. Everywhere she looked, she saw lights and tinsel and bows and Santas. He even had a tree with lights sitting in the middle of the lot. *Good luck with that, Ralph.* She wondered how long that would last before someone knocked it over.

Cara pushed open the door to the store and froze at the sight of a gun pointed in her direction.

"Stop right there." The man behind the weapon narrowed his eyes onto hers.

"I am stopped." Oops, why did that come out of her mouth? Maybe Mr. Perkins bad attitude rubbed off on her.

He glared at her. "Don't get smart with me lady. I'm the one holding the gun and I'll use it if I have to."

Cara stared at the man. She didn't recognize him, but he didn't look like any robber she'd ever seen on TV or in pictures. Dressed in clean slacks and a pullover shirt, his dark hair appeared to be recently trimmed and his face newly shaved. He looked like he belonged in one of the offices around town, not robbing the local Grab It 'N Go.

She looked around for Ralph Meredith. He stood behind the counter with both hands raised over his head. He blinked at Cara and shook his head as if to say, 'don't do anything stupid.'

The guy waved the gun at her. "Lady, move over by the counter where I can see both of you."

She let go of the door she had been holding open and walked over to stand next to Ralph.

He pointed the gun at Ralph. "I do not want any trouble. I just want to hear you say the words."

Cara turned and looked at Ralph, then back at the gunman. "You're holding a gun on us because you want Ralph to say… what?"

"He knows what to say."

Cara turned back to the store owner. "For Pete's sake, Ralph, say the words."

"No ma'am, Miss Cara. They're not

true. I would be lying."

She sighed and looked at the shooter. "What is it you want him to say?"

"It's not really any of your business."

Frustration swept over Cara. In the first place, this didn't feel like a real holdup. Although the man did have a gun, he wasn't stealing anything. Secondly, she doubted he would really shoot either one of them. He didn't seem the type. Add in the fact that she was exhausted, and she didn't much care if he did shoot her.

She put one hand on her hip and glared at him. "I would say it is *my* business since you're holding me hostage."

The man frowned. "I'm not holding you hostage. I wouldn't do anything like that."

Cara laughed at the pure craziness of the situation. This guy couldn't be serious.

"Ma'am, please be quiet."

Something about the way he spoke stopped her. He wasn't some bum off the street. He was polite, soft-spoken, and well-dressed. For some reason, his actions convinced her he wouldn't shoot.

She turned to Ralph. "I don't know what's going on between the two of you, but I have a life to get on with, not to mention that I've had a rough week so far. Why don't you just say the words so I can get my food and go home?"

Ralph shook his head.

She turned back to the gunman. "You know you're going to jail for this. It's not worth it."

"That's for me to decide."

She took a deep breath. "Well, if you have to shoot, just go ahead and shoot, I'm leaving." She started for the door.

"No, don't shoot her." Ralph's voice boomed over the store. "I'll say the words." He cleared his throat.

Cara turned around. The gunman stood closer now with the gun pointed at her. She took a second look at it. Up close, it didn't look like a real gun. She took a step toward the man.

"Hold it right there, ma'am."

"Is that a real gun?"

His eyes widened. "Are you crazy? Of course, it's a real gun."

She shook her head. "I don't think it is." She inched forward. "Who are you? I've never seen you around here before."

"It's not important who I am."

Cara turned to Ralph. "I need a barbecue sandwich and some coleslaw. Can you get it for me, please?"

Ralph arched one eyebrow. "I think we better do what he says, Cara."

She glanced around the area where they stood. A display of rubber balls sat on the counter. Without another thought, she grabbed one and threw it at the gunman. He stepped backward into a candy display. He threw up his arms to grab something for support. When he did, the gun flew out of his hand and landed on the floor.

Cara lunged for the gun and picked it up. She laughed. "Just as I thought, it's plastic." She marched over to the red-faced gunman who lay on the floor surrounded by candy canes and chocolate reindeer.

She pointed the gun at him. "Bang, bang." She shook her head. "Of all the crazy stunts. I hope they lock you up. You're nuts, you know it?"

She turned to Ralph. "Call the police and have him arrested."

Ralph frowned. "It's really plastic?"

She handed him the gun and stomped toward the door.

"Ma'am, wait a minute. I need to explain."

Cara pushed open the door and strode toward her car, her reason for going to the store completely forgotten. She climbed inside and looked up to see the gunman coming toward her. She quickly locked the doors and started the engine. He tapped on the window. She looked at him and shook her head, then put the car in drive. When she glanced in her rearview mirror, he was standing in the middle of the parking lot staring after her.

As she drove home, she wondered what words the gunman had wanted Ralph to say. Whatever they were, it had been important enough to the stranger to pull a dumb stunt that could get him arrested.

Chapter 2

Thanksgiving Day, November 24

The first thing Cara thought of when she awoke on Thanksgiving morning was the gunman at the Grab It 'N Go. The whole thing was so crazy it could have been a dream or a B-rated TV movie. Except for one thing, she witnessed the whole weird incident. She wondered if Ralph reported the nut.

Her cell rang and she picked it up.

"Hi Mom."

"Good morning. Just wanted to check with you about the salad you promised to bring."

Cara closed her eyes and slapped her forehead. With all the stress at work, she had forgotten all about it. She would have to make a quick dash to Lawton's Supermarket. They were only open until noon today due to the holiday.

"I'll bring it. Anything else?"

"No, that's it. Greg and Haley are bringing a pecan pie and rolls. I've already baked pumpkin and chocolate pies. Everything else is in the oven or fridge. We eat at 2:00 o'clock. What time can we expect you?"

"I'll be there at one."

"Okay, see you then. By the way, we're having some other people join us today." Her mom disconnected the call.

What? Who? She stared at the phone in confusion. Usually just family showed up on Thanksgiving—her parents, her brother and sister-in-law, Aunt Mavis, and Grandmother Clara. She wondered who the "other people" could be.

Cara climbed out of bed and padded to the kitchen. She made a list of the ingredients for broccoli salad while her coffee brewed. Then she carried her mug outside and sat on the patio. It was a perfect fall Day with crisp morning air and golden leaves that swirled from their lofty perches on sparse tree limbs to touch the ground below. Just the kind of day Brandt enjoyed. Her mood immediately swung from contentment to bitter resentment.

We could be enjoying this together if you hadn't abandoned me. How could you say you loved me and hurt me this way?

Tears stung her eyes, and she closed them against the pain. It had been seventeen months and she still felt the ache of Brandt's actions. When she opened them again, the day had lost some of its brilliance. She tossed the last of her coffee on the brown grass and went inside where she pulled on jeans and a tee shirt and ran a brush through her shoulder-length blonde hair. Ten minutes later, she climbed into her car and headed for Lawton's Supermarket to buy the needed salad items. As she drove, she noticed that many Redwood citizens had their homes ready for Christmas. Never mind that leaves were still falling and today was Thanksgiving, they had already plunged into the holiday pandemonium. She dreaded the days ahead with all the parties, decorating, and shopping. She had no Christmas spirit and didn't care to be involved in the festivities. Another thing Brandt yanked from her heart as he disappeared from her life. *God, why did you let that happen to me? Do you even care?*

She had reservations about Christmas.

Those feelings started the first Christmas after Brandt had left her waiting at the church on their wedding day that hot summer day in July. He never showed up or called. He simply disappeared out of her life, never to be heard from again. Bitterness gripped her. Hurt and humiliated beyond words she left town for a few weeks until her mom and dad convinced her that the good people in Redwood, Texas knew what a jerk Brandt Peters was. In fact, she seemed to be the only person who didn't know it until it was too late.

Not that her family and friends hadn't tried to warn her about him, they had, but she had refused to listen to anything negative about Brandt. He had deceived her, charmed her, and lied to her. She had been completely mesmerized by him. When her parents and brother tried to talk her out of marrying him, she moved out of the house. They tried to convince her right up to the day before the wedding. When she accused them of trying to ruin the most important day of her life, they finally backed off.

So, she came home and went to work for Sam Perkins. It had been hard those first months. She could see the pity in everyone's eyes when they walked into the office or ran into her while shopping or on Sundays at church. Some of them felt it necessary to tell her they were sorry for what Brandt had done. She just wanted to forget about it, and she wanted everyone else to forget too.

When Christmas rolled around five months later, she had no holiday spirit whatsoever. She went through the motions of helping her family celebrate, but her heart wasn't in it.

Cara swallowed the now familiar ache, shoved it back into its hiding place in her heart and pulled into the parking lot of the superm arket.

"White Christmas" blared over the intercom, and she sighed to herself. Why couldn't they wait just one more day before starting the holiday music? Thanksgiving seemed to get rushed through with all the Christmas hype. It had long been her family's favorite holiday. Besides, the chances of having a white Christmas in Texas were slim to none.

She grabbed a basket and headed for the produce section. The vegetable bins lay almost empty, but she managed to find the fresh broccoli, red grapes, and green onions she needed for her salad. Heading toward the isle where the red wine vinegar was located, she rounded the corner and came face to face with the fake gunman from the day before. She stopped and frowned at him.

"You should be in jail."

His eyes widened and a sheepish look crossed his face. "Ma'am, I'm sorry about yesterday. Let me explain."

She held up her hand. "I don't want to hear any crazy explanations from someone who carries a gun around to threaten people." She heard a few gasps from the other shoppers in the aisle.

He looked around at the other customers. "It was a plastic gun, not a real one."

She frowned at him again.

He sighed deeply. "I know. It was a huge mistake on my part."

"A mistake? If I had been in Ralph's shoes, I would have filed charges against you."

He took a step closer. "Please. Let me explain."

"No. I don't want to hear anything you have to say." She pulled her basket tight against her as if it could shield her and stepped around him.

She hurried down the aisle and around

the end of a display then stopped. Oh, for heaven's sake. The red wine vinegar was on the aisle she had just left, but she didn't want anything to do with that bizarre gunman. She waited a few seconds, then peered around the display of stuffing mix to make sure he was gone. She grabbed a bottle of vinegar and hurried to the checkout.

As she waited in line, she kept glancing around for him, but he had disappeared. Why on earth didn't Ralph have him picked up and put in jail? Would his actions be considered a crime? She set her items on the counter and waited as the cashier rang them up, then paid and left the store.

Back home, she washed the vegetables and started the salad. The house seemed unusually quiet today. She reached over and pushed the power button on the radio she kept on the kitchen counter.

The voice of the local DJ, Johnny Sutter, filled the room. "And now for your holiday listening enjoyment, here's George Strait singing "Christmas Cookies." Well, if she had to listen to Christmas music today, she didn't mind as long as the DJ chose one of her favorite artists. She hummed along as she chopped the vegetables into bite-sized pieces.

Brandt had liked him too. He had taken her to see George Strait in concert. That night he had proposed.

Stop. I will not let you ruin my day, Brandt Peters.

She pushed the thought of him out of her mind. Thankfully, the song ended. She tried to think about something else, anything, even the crazy gunman.

Who was he anyway? She had never seen him in Redwood before. In a town this small she pretty much knew everyone that lived here. When a stranger came to town, they stuck out like a black sheep in a herd. What had he been doing in Ralph's store and what did he want Ralph to say? Maybe she would go by there tomorrow and ask Ralph.

When she finished the salad, she placed it in the fridge and went to change her clothes. Her mother had mentioned guests, so faded jeans and a tee shirt wouldn't do. She dressed in a pair of black slacks, a white sweater and added a gold chain.

An hour later, she pulled her silver Nissan into her parents' driveway and parked behind her brother's red SUV. A white car sat in front of the house. That must be the company her mother had mentioned unless Aunt

Mavis had a new car which was highly unlikely since she had given up driving except in an emergency. Retrieving the bowl of salad from the backseat, she hurried up the steps and pushed open the kitchen door. The fragrance of her mother's Thanksgiving cooking filled the room. She inhaled the fragrant aroma and her stomach growled.

"There you are." Her mother came across the room with outstretched arms.

Cara set the bowl of salad on the counter, hugged her mother close then whispered in her ear. "Whose white car is out front?"

"Come and see." Her mother pulled her toward the den.

Her brother, Greg, grabbed her for a hug as soon as she stepped into the room. Her sister-in-law, Haley, came right behind him, and her dad next. You would think they hadn't seen each other in years, when in fact they had all spent a week together in September on a family vacation.

Her dad slipped his arm around her shoulders. "Come greet our guests, Cara."

She looked to where he pointed and stared directly into the face of the crazy gunman from Ralph's store. Cara stared at him in shocked surprise. He shuffled his feet and looked away.

She bit her lip to keep from asking why he had invaded her parents' house. Next to him stood Paul Freeman, the minister from Redwood Community Church and his wife, Carol.

Cara plastered on a half-smile. "Welcome to our family Thanksgiving."

The minister clapped the gunman on the back. "Cara, I'd like you to meet my brother, Joshua, Josh for short. "He's here to spend the holidays with us. Your folks said it would be okay to bring him along so here we are."

Just my luck. The same guy who holds me at gunpoint on Wednesday comes to my family Thanksgiving on Thursday.

Chapter 3

Cara tried to speak, but her throat felt frozen. She couldn't believe this man sat in her parents' den about to eat turkey and dressing with her family.

He spoke first. "It's nice to meet you, Cara." His eyes pleaded for mercy.

She took a deep breath and opened her mouth, but she was rendered speechless by the sight of him.

Paul touched her shoulder and spoke in a lowered tone. "Is something wrong, Cara?"

She glanced at his furrowed brow. He was clearly puzzled by her reaction. In the background, she heard her mother's voice.

"We're ready to eat. Everyone come to the dining room."

Cara swallowed hard in an effort to speak but the sight of him left her speechless. Despite the fact, this Josh was the last person she wanted to share Thanksgiving dinner with, he had been invited to her parents' home, and she wouldn't do anything to spoil this day for them.

She shook her head and turned to Paul. "No everything is fine. I'm glad you could join us today."

Her mother's voice cut into their conversation. "Cara, could you help me for a moment?"

"Excuse me, I better see what Mother needs." She hurried out of the den and into the kitchen.

Her mother frowned. "Are you feeling okay? You look a little pale." Her mother laid her hand on Cara's forehead. "You don't seem to have a temp, but your color isn't good."

"I'm fine, Mother." She frowned.

"Then what's wrong? Is something bothering you?" She slipped an arm around Cara's waist. "You're not letting the memory of Brandt spoil today, are you?"

She might as well admit to it, or her mother wouldn't let it go. "I'm just surprised at the extra guests today. It caught me off guard. It's always been just us."

Her mother smiled. "I'm sorry. I should have let you know sooner that they were coming. I didn't know it would matter that much. While we were at the community Thanksgiving service last night, we found out that Paul and Carol were going to be alone today. We couldn't stand the thought of them being without family, so we invited them. We didn't know his brother would be joining us until this morning when Paul called." Mom shook her head. "It's okay, though. The more, the merrier, I always say." She picked up a sweet potato casserole and a bowl of seasoned green beans and headed for the dining room. "Bring your salad and the rolls."

After the minister said grace, her dad carved the turkey as the room filled with chatter. Cara stole a glance at Josh the gunman chatting with Greg as though they were old friends. Only he didn't look like a gunman now. Well, he hadn't looked like a gunman yesterday either, but he had that silly toy gun in his hand then and made threatening remarks. Now he acted like a normal person.

He glanced up and their eyes met. She glared at him. He had the same pleading look for mercy as he had earlier. She turned to her

Aunt Mavis sitting next to her.

"How have you been? Is your health better?" She could still feel his eyes on her, but she refused to look at him. Of all the nerve, showing up at her family holiday. Of course, he hadn't known this was her family, but it would serve him right if she didn't show him the mercy he wanted and instead asked him about his plastic gun right here in front of everyone. She forced her attention back to her aunt who was talking about her bad knees.

"Cara."

She looked up at the sound of her name.

Paul Freeman smiled at her from across the table. "I wondered if we might elicit your help with decorating the church this weekend. We're running a bit behind this year. Everyone else in town seems to be ready for the Christmas season." He smiled. "Your dad tells me you're good at decorating."

She sensed Josh's eyes on her, but she focused on the minister. Just as she started to refuse, her dad broke in.

"She always seems to know just how to arrange everything to make it look good. I'm sure she'll be glad to help."

At that moment, she felt like kicking her dad under the table. The last thing she wanted was to be anywhere near where Josh might be in close proximity, but she swallowed her refusal and nodded. Everyone at the table eyed her, waiting for her answer. "I guess I could help. When do you need me?"

"We're meeting tomorrow morning at nine."

The rest of the meal became a blur to Cara. She couldn't enjoy the food, conversation, or company with the would-be gunman sitting across the table from her. She responded whenever someone spoke to her, but otherwise she sat in miserable silence, wishing it would all end. If it had been her house, she would have exposed him without a second thought, but her parents were some of the most giving, kindest, generous people she knew and she would never disrespect them in their own home in front of guests. The sound of his voice jolted her out of her bubble of silence.

"I've never had broccoli salad before, but this is really delicious."

Cara flinched but didn't say anything.

Her mother spoke up. "Cara made the broccoli salad. And you're right, it is delicious." She smiled at Cara. "Thanks for bringing it sweetheart."

Cara smiled at her mom. "You're welcome."

When everyone finished eating, the men headed to the den to watch football while the women cleared the table. Relief washed through Cara to finally be free of his pleading eyes. In the kitchen, her mom handed her a plastic container.

"There are plenty of leftovers. Fill this and take it home with you."

"Thanks, Mom." She accepted the container and began filling it with her favorite dishes.

When the table had been cleared and the kitchen cleaned, the women all made their way to the den where the men had gathered. As soon as they entered the room, Paul Freeman stood.

"We have enjoyed ourselves immensely today, but we are expected somewhere else later this evening, so we need to be going." He thanked her parents and began making the rounds shaking hands and saying goodbye, his wife and brother in tow.

Before they reached her, Cara slipped out and went to the bathroom where she stayed until she heard the door close. When she came out, her parents were sitting in the den with

Greg and Haley. The four of them looked up as she came into the room.

Her dad spoke first. "Cara, girl, what's bothering you? You were quiet during dinner which is very unlike you."

"Yeah, I noticed it too." Greg arched an eyebrow at her.

Haley wrinkled her nose. "I think it had something to do with Josh. It almost felt like they knew each other."

Her dad sat forward in the recliner. "Had you met him before?"

She shrugged. "Maybe."

Her mother squinted at her. "Out with it."

Cara raised her hands in surrender. "Okay, okay, but you're not going to believe me when I tell you." For the next few minutes, she filled them in on what had happened at Ralph's Grab It 'N Go. When she finished, they wore a mixture of disbelief and skepticism on their faces.

"If you don't believe me, ask Ralph."

We believe you," her mother said. "It's just that it's so weird. Why would he do such a thing?"

Greg shrugged. "He sure didn't seem like that kind of person today."

"Trust me, it happened. I was there."

Her mother frowned. "And it really was just a plastic gun?"

Cara nodded. "Yes, I picked it up and looked at it."

Her dad shook his head. "One thing for sure, I'm going to ask Paul about it. That's not a good thing for the church or the town."

"He sure put up a front today." Greg glanced around the room. "Next time, it may be a real gun."

Cara shivered. She hadn't even thought about there being a next time.

Chapter 4

Friday, November 25

When her alarm rang at seven the next morning, Cara threw back the covers and climbed out of bed. She would have preferred to sleep in after three tiring days at work, but she had promised the minister she would help decorate the church. She wasn't looking forward to it.

At eight forty-five, armed with a travel mug full of coffee, she backed out of her garage and headed for the church. She arrived to find a handful of members in the fellowship hall laughing and talking. She didn't feel quite that excited about the project, but she joined them anyway. She looked around for Josh, but he was nowhere in sight. Knowing him, he was probably out committing another robbery with his plastic gun.

The minister asked for their attention and began delegating responsibilities to each person. When he came to Cara, he smiled.

"Glad you could join us. I'm pairing you with Josh. The two of you can set up the manger scene in the front yard.

She looked around and her stomach lurched. He leaned against the wall in the back of the room. He waved at her and smiled. She turned her back. Everything in her screamed 'no, I will not work with him,' but how could she refuse in front of all these people, her friends, her parent's friends, people she had known all her life.

Josh walked over to her. "Looks like we're on the same team."

She gave him an icy stare. He drew back as if struck, then turned and walked over to Paul. She followed, wondering what he would say to his brother, but he simply asked, "Where's the nativity?"

They carried the wooden figures and animals out to the front yard, but they both had to carry the heavy manger. For the next hour, they worked silently setting up the scene in front of the church. When they finished, Josh stood back and looked at their project.

"We make a pretty good team." His lips attempted a tight smile.

"You're wrong about that." She shook her head. "I only worked with you because your brother put us together." She rested her hands on her hips. "What I want to know is what you were doing at Ralph's Wednesday holding a gun—correction, a plastic gun—and threatening us with it."

He sighed. "I wasn't really threatening you."

"Then what do you call it? You said you would shoot me if I moved."

His face turned red, and the color spread down his neck. "I wouldn't really shoot you or anyone else for that matter. To be honest with you, it was a bet I made with a friend of mine."

Cara glared at him. "A bet? What kind of a bet?"

Josh dipped his head and looked at the ground. "I hitched a ride with an old college buddy and when we hit town, he began laughing about how quaint and sleepy it seemed. 'Time to rev things up a bit, huh?' He bet me one hundred dollars I couldn't pull off a fake robbery without getting caught. Like an idiot, I followed him into that store." Josh glanced away, as if embarrassed to say more. Then he swallowed. "No one else was in there. Just us and the clerk." He shrugged. "That's all there was to it. Didn't you notice the guy standing over in the corner with his phone filming it?"

Anger surged through Cara. If they hadn't been standing on the front lawn of the church in full view of anyone passing by, she would have picked up one of the wooden nativity figures and hit him with it.

"Did Ralph know about this bet?"

He shook his head. "Not at first. I told him later. He got pretty mad."

"Do you blame him? It would have served you right if he had called the police and had you arrested. I'm a good mind to call them anyway and tell them what you did."

Josh's face paled. "Please don't do that. It would embarrass Paul and Carol."

"You should have thought of that before you pulled such a stunt." With that, she turned and hurried to her car."

"Wait, Cara. I'm sorry."

She ignored his plea and slid into the driver's seat. Her hands trembled as she put the key into the ignition, but when the engine started, she pulled away just as he stepped up to the window.

Chapter 5

Josh watched as Cara pulled out of the church parking lot. He felt like kicking himself. He didn't blame her for being mad. He had realized yesterday at her parent's house just how much it had infuriated her to be a part of his and Adam's prank.

The worst part? Realizing yesterday that her family attended Paul's church and he had done something that could reflect badly on Paul and the church. Shame swirled through him at what he had allowed himself to get involved in—college buddy and good friend, or not.

His brother didn't deserve trouble and neither did Cara or Ralph. They were all good people. *Why, oh why did I agree to hitch a ride with Adam as he travelled to his folks' house in Dallas. The guy's trouble with a capital T.*

Little did he know the prettiest woman he'd seen in ages would walk into that store, right in the middle of their boyish prank. He had blown his chance at getting to know her better. Even when she was mad, it didn't diminish her beauty. *How you gonna fix this one, huh?* He kicked his shoe into the asphalt parking lot. He wondered if there was anything he could do to make it up to her. He shook his head at her disappearing car.

Josh turned and walked back toward the church. He noticed that one of the wise men had fallen and walked over to pick it up. He stared at it for a moment before placing it back in the ground. *Wish someone could pick me up and put me back in place. You pulled a foolish stunt, Josh Freeman. You're not a wise man at all.*

He didn't hear his brother walk up behind him.

"Hey, Josh, where's Cara? They're serving hot chocolate and cookies in the fellowship hall."

Josh's face grew warm. "She's already left."

Paul frowned. "She didn't stay too long, did she?"

Josh shook his head. "She seemed a bit upset about something."

"That's too bad. I was hoping the two of you could become friends."

"I don't think there's much of a chance of that."

"I noticed the two of you acted strange yesterday. Did you know each other before?"

Josh shook his head. "No, but we had met once before, and it wasn't a good meeting."

Paul cleared his throat. "Do you want to talk about it?"

Josh shook his head. "I'd rather not. Maybe later."

Paul laid his arm across his younger brother's shoulders. "Whenever you're ready, you know you can share whatever you like with me. Now how about some hot chocolate?"

"Thanks, but I think I'll go inside and practice my guitar for a while. If I'm going to be a part of the orchestra, I need to brush up on some of the music."

Paul headed toward the fellowship hall and Josh stepped inside the quiet sanctuary. He walked to the front, picked up his guitar and began strumming softly. Without warning, his eyes filled with tears. He stopped playing and leaned his head onto the instrument. Memories of the past few years flashed before his eyes: The lies to keep himself out of trouble, the drunken parties, the pranks he had been a part of, pranks that had hurt people. He felt almost sick to his stomach thinking about all he had allowed himself to get involved in.

"God, I've made a mess of my life. I've lived for the good times. I've thought of nothing but myself and what I wanted out of life. I need to change my way of living. Forgive me for hurting Cara and Ralph with my childish prank."

He sat there in silence for a few moments, as a warm peace settled over him, then he began to play again, closing his eyes and letting the melody soothe his broken spirit.

Chapter 6

Cara pulled into her parents' driveway willing herself to calm down before she went inside and talked to her dad. He had mentioned telling the minister about Josh's actions, but that was before she found out it was a prank. It still made her furious to think someone would play such a heartless joke on other people, but she didn't want Paul and Carol Freeman to be hurt or embarrassed by what Josh had done.

She took a deep breath and climbed out of the car. Her dad opened the front just as she reached for the doorknob.

"Hey, Sweetheart, finished decorating the church already?"

She nodded. "Well, my part was helping set up the nativity and we did that."

"So, what brings you here? You're

usually shopping or getting your nails done or whatever it is you girls do in your free time."

"I have something to tell you about Josh."

He nodded. "Come on in, your mother needs to hear it too."

Cara followed him inside. From where she entered, she could see a green tree with gold balls and red twinkling lights in the corner of the den.

"I see you've already put your tree up."

Her dad grinned. "Your mother asked me to bring it down from the attic while we were eating breakfast. She worked on it all morning."

They found her mother in the kitchen heating up Thanksgiving leftovers.

"This is a nice surprise." Her mother wiped her hands on a towel and hugged her. "How about having lunch with us?"

"Sure, I'd love to."

Her dad pulled out a chair at the table and sat down. "Cara has something to tell us about Paul's brother, Josh."

Her mother cocked her head to one side. "Not more trouble I hope." She handed Cara three plates.

Cara set them on the table, then turned

to her parents.

"Dad, yesterday you mentioned talking to Paul about what Josh had done. I'm not sure that's a good idea."

Her dad arched his brows. "Yesterday, you were angry about his stunt."

Cara nodded. "And today I found out that's exactly what it was. A college buddy of his bet him one hundred dollars that he couldn't pull off a fake robbery without getting caught. His buddy even filmed it with his cell phone."

Her mother set what was left of the sweet potato casserole on the table. "That's pretty childish."

"He asked that we not tell Paul because he doesn't want them to be embarrassed. As angry as I've been and still am, maybe we shouldn't say anything."

Her dad sighed and shook his head. "I guess you're right. Why don't we let it ride for the time being and just wait and see how he acts from this point on. If he continues to pull these kinds of stunts, then I think we need to say something."

Cara's mother set the rest of the food on the table and took her place. "Let's just hope it's a one-time thing and he never does it again."

Her dad said grace and they filled their plates. The food tasted better than it had the day before. Cara hadn't enjoyed it much yesterday because of Josh's presence. Today she savored every bite of her mother's delicious cooking.

When they finished lunch, Cara placed the dishes in the dishwasher and helped her mother clean the kitchen, then she left for home. As she went out the door, she glanced at her parents' tree one more time and saw it a tad differently. It did brighten the room. *Maybe I'll get my own out of the closet and decorate it while I feel motivated.*

It wasn't much fun pulling it out of the box and setting it up, but once she had it put together, she got out the lights and ornaments. To her dismay, she only had one string of lights that worked. That meant she had to go buy more. She grabbed her keys and purse and headed to Farmer's Pharmacy.

Doris waved at her from the checkout counter. She had several customers waiting in line, so Cara wandered around the store until she found the lights. She picked up three strings and placed them in her basket. Next to the light display a beautiful selection of ornaments caught her eye. On impulse, she decided to redo her tree and began selecting ornaments and garland.

"Looks like someone is getting ready to decorate a tree."

Cara froze at the sound of that voice. She glanced up to see Josh standing on the other side of the display.

He smiled at her. "Am I right? Are you setting up your tree today?"

"Yes."

"I'll be glad to help you. I'm pretty good at stringing lights."

"No, thank you."

"Please. I would love to help."

Cara shook her head and repeated it a bit more firmly. "No, thank you." She went back to selecting a few more ornaments. Not hearing a response, she glanced up to see if he had left.

He stood there with a despondent look on his face as if he might burst into tears although she didn't think he would. That wasn't too characteristic of the men she knew.

He swallowed and cleared his throat. "Cara, I'm sorry about the prank I pulled at Ralphs. I wish we could put it behind us and be friends. Is there any chance of that?"

She wasn't ready to forgive him. Except for Brandt's abandonment, he had made her angrier than she had ever been before. Okay, perhaps the pain she still felt from Brandt's past actions kept her from reaching out to Josh, but he deserved it. He had purposely played a joke on innocent people.

Paul's recent sermon on forgiveness flashed through her mind. She took a deep breath. The right thing to do would be to forgive him and accept his offer of friendship. He had nothing to do with the past or what had happened to her. But she just couldn't. Not yet anyway.

"Look, maybe you are sorry for what you did, but it was heartless, cruel, and just saying you're sorry doesn't cut it. Maybe someday I can forgive you, but not now." He nodded and walked away; his shoulders slumped in dejection. He looked so sad, she almost felt sorry for him. Almost.

As she drove toward home, she had a sudden thought and headed for Ralph's Grab It 'N Go. He was behind the counter talking to a customer when she walked in. He nodded at her, and she smiled. While he finished with the other person, she walked over to the restored candy display and chose a bag of mini chocolate bars for the candy dish at home.

After the other customer finished his business, Cara walked to the counter.

"Hi, had any more robberies lately, Ralph?" She gave him a quick grin.

Ralph rolled his eyes. "No and I hope I don't." He squinted at her. "How are you doing after our little escapade on Wednesday?"

She laid the bag of candy on the counter. "I'm fine, but I'm still mad at him for pulling that prank on us. Not only that, but I keep running into him everywhere I go." She handed Ralph a five-dollar bill. "Did you know that he's Paul Freeman's brother?"

Ralph arched both eyebrows in surprise. "No, I didn't." He shook his head. "He's sure nothing like his brother."

"By the way, what were the words he wanted you to say? Must have been something pretty bad for you to refuse with a gun on you." She laughed.

Ralph chuckled. "I didn't know it was a toy at the time, but I wasn't going to state something that's false, not even for a gunman. I almost gave in, but thanks to you and that rubber ball, I didn't say them."

"So, what were the words?"

"He wanted me to say that I don't believe in Christmas."

Cara frowned. "That's it?"

Ralph sighed. "I know it doesn't seem like a big deal, but it's the principle of the thing. I do believe in Christmas and what it stands for—the reason we celebrate it. Denying Christmas would be like denying my faith as far as I'm concerned."

Ralph's words felt like cold water had been thrown in her face. Is that what she had been doing? Denying her faith? Allowing her bitterness toward Brandt to seep over into her relationship with God? Surely not.

She shrugged. "I guess you're right. I just never thought about it in that way."

Cara paid for her candy and drove home, but she had lost interest in decorating the tree today. Ralph's words kept ringing in her ears. She couldn't get away from them. She switched on the TV, but the screen filled with commercials for the best gifts, movies, food, and clothes for the season. She switched channels and the Grinch smiled his evil smile as he stole Christmas. She turned the TV off and tossed the remote on the coffee table.

So much for trying to forget about the season and what it meant. Nothing on that blue screen could convince her that she should celebrate. People made too much of Christmas. Why not just forget the whole thing? After all, it was just another day full of pointless traditions. "But I love those traditions," she said aloud to the empty room.

Is that what Christmas has become to you? Just a lot of traditions?

"It used to mean more before you allowed Brandt to hurt me."

Are you going to allow him to influence your relationship with me?

Cara closed her eyes. She didn't want to hear anymore. She wondered if some part of her still loved Brandt even after his treatment of her.

He will never love you the way I do.

Chapter 7

Sunday, November 27

The first person Cara saw at church on Sunday morning was Josh. He got out of the white car she had seen parked in front of her parents' house on Thanksgiving Day. It hadn't occurred to her someone like him would be at church today. Not someone who walked around threatening and scaring people. But then of course, he was the minister's brother. He would have to show up to make a good impression. She watched him walk toward the building. He looked sharp in gray slacks and jacket. Not bad looking for a prankster.

She waited until he went inside before getting out of her car to enter the church. Her parents already sat in their usual spot, so she scooted in next to her mom. Soon after, Greg and Haley joined them. They exchanged small talk until the service started.

The choir opened with a lively rendition of "Go Tell It on the Mountain." Cara caught herself tapping her foot to the music. When they finished, Paul Freeman stepped to the platform.

"I would like to introduce someone to you this morning." He turned toward the orchestra and nodded. Josh stood. "This is my brother, Josh. He'll be with us through the holiday season." He chuckled. "Who knows, we might convince him to make Redwood his home."

Everyone clapped except Cara. If only she could put the picture of him holding a gun—although a plastic one—out of her mind, she might be able to feel a little more friendly toward him. The clapping died down. Paul spoke again.

"Josh is going to bless us with a musical number this morning. I know you will enjoy it. He's quite an accomplished guitarist."

Cara stared as he walked to the front carrying a guitar. He looked like a normal person, nothing like the gunman of a few days ago. Taller than Paul and well built—the word sharp flashed through her mind.

He smiled at the congregation. "Thank you for that warm welcome. I'll be playing a medley of hymns this morning. You shouldn't have any trouble recognizing them because they're old ones we all grew up with." He strummed an opening chord and then began playing.

She had to admit he was good. The instrument seemed to come alive under his touch. He had a way of making it sound as though he was an orchestra all by himself. She closed her eyes and let the music refresh her, energizing her after the frustrations of the past week. When his medley ended, she felt a little sorry he decided not to continue. She glanced at her dad for his reaction. He arched an eyebrow and nodded at her.

Josh returned to his place with the other musicians and the service continued, but she only heard parts of it because she kept sneaking glances at Josh. Not because she had forgiven him, but something kept drawing her attention his way. She wished he weren't so handsome. It would be easier to ignore him if she could only see him as the wild gunman at Ralph's Grab It 'N Go. Not as the handsome, talented, smartly dressed musician sitting on stage now.

Chapter 8

Monday, November 28

Mondays got a lot of flak about being bad or blue, but Cara had always felt Mondays gave her a fresh start. She wanted to forget about last week and go forward. In addition, Sam was on his cruise and the work environment would be calm and pleasant. Or so she thought. The moment she walked into Perkins Law Firm, Olivia and Emma rushed over to her.

"I can't believe what happened at Ralph's last Wednesday." Olivia shook her head. "When I saw that video on Facebook this morning I almost flipped out."

The blood in Cara's veins turned ice cold. "What video?"

"The one with the gunman holding you and Ralph hostage." Emma held her cell phone out for Cara to see. There was Josh pointing the plastic gun as she and Ralph held their hands up in the air.

Cara closed her eyes to blot out the embarrassing video playing across the screen. She could hear her own voice in the background and Josh answering her.

Emma touched her shoulder. "Cara, are you okay?"

She opened her eyes. "I can't believe he posted that video on Facebook for the whole town to see."

Olivia frowned. "Who? The robber?"

"Yes, but he wasn't really a robber. He played a prank on Ralph although we didn't know it at the time."

Emma pointed at the video. "But he had a gun."

"It wasn't a real gun. It was a plastic toy." She sighed in exasperation. If she could get her hands on Josh Freeman right now, she would strangle him. Brandt's stunt had already made her the subject of too much attention in Redwood. She had just begun to feel comfortable living here and seeing everyone in public. Now this. She couldn't believe Josh had been gutsy enough to post the video after he had been introduced at church yesterday by his brother, the minister, and then played the guitar so beautifully. And he had said he was sorry. But he wasn't really, was he? What a smooth liar. She felt sick to her stomach and placed her hand over her middle as if to make the feeling subside.

Olivia slid her cell phone inside her jacket pocket. "Are you okay?"

Cara shook her head. "I can't believe this whole wretched situation. Makes me sick to my stomach."

Emma perched on the corner of her desk. "If you're not feeling well, we can handle things here if you want to go home."

Olivia nodded. "Yes, with Sam out of the office, there's not much to do."

Cara took a deep breath. She refused to let Josh get the best of her. "No, I'm okay. I'll stay. Besides, what if Sam calls to see what we're doing."

Emma shrugged. "We'll just tell him you're sick."

"Thanks, but I'll make it." At least she hoped she would.

She opened her laptop and logged onto Facebook to see how many people had already viewed the post. She glanced at the number of Likes, almost afraid to look, and the sick feeling intensified. Thirty-five viewers had already responded, five of them had shared the video with their friends. She clicked on the icon to see who they were. Most of them were names she didn't recognize, but some of the most prominent people in Redwood had also viewed the video. She scanned through the names, looking for Paul or Carol Freeman, then her parents, and then Greg and Haley. None of them were listed. She sighcd with relief until she saw Sam's name.

The phone on her desk rang and she almost jumped out of her chair. She answered the call, her heart pounding.

"Cara, this is Josh."

She didn't give him time to say anything else.

"How could you? Wasn't it enough that you threatened Ralph and me and tried to scare us? Now you've posted the video. What kind of person are you? Do you get pleasure out of hurting other people? And you had the nerve to get up in church yesterday and play your guitar, acting like a good old boy. You make me sick."

Without another word, she hung up the

phone, laid her head on her desk, and burst into tears. Olivia and Emma rushed to her side immediately, patting her on the back, trying to console her. The chime on the office door rang. She grabbed a tissue and raised her head to see who entered the office. The man stared at her, puzzled for a moment.

Olivia came to the rescue. "Can I help you, sir?"

He pulled a business card out of his pocket. "I'm Jess Porter with Better Investments. I'm looking for Sam Perkins."

Olivia smiled warmly as she stepped toward him. "I'm sorry, Mr. Perkins is out of town this week. Would you care to leave a message?"

The man continued to sneak glances at Cara as he talked with Olivia. "Just give him my card and tell him I'll be in touch." He walked to the door and took one last look at Cara.

"You look familiar." He squinted at her. "Do I know you from somewhere?"

Cara shook her head. "No, I've never seen you before."

The man shrugged and left.

Fresh tears rose to her eyes. "He probably saw the Facebook post and that's why I look familiar to him."

Olivia looked at the business card in her hand. "He's not from around here. He has an Oklahoma address. I wouldn't let it bother me if I were you."

Before she could respond, the phone rang again. She could hear Sam chuckling on the other end. "Cara, just saw the Facebook post. I bet you're mad at your friend, Adam. for posting that video."

"Adam? Who's Adam? How did you see the post?" Cara asked, dreading to hear his answer.

"A friend of mine shared it on his timeline. I think he got it from somewhere else. It says here that the would-be robber had a plastic gun." Sam hung up but not before she heard him laughing.

Josh's words came rushing back to her. *Didn't you notice the guy standing over in the corner with his phone? He was filming it.*

The sick feeling in her stomach returned mixed with regret this time. *Josh didn't post it.* Adam the college buddy was the culprit. She had just given Josh a piece of her mind, said some pretty rough things to him, and he didn't have anything to do with posting the video.

Shame swept over her. She had done it

again—opened her mouth without thinking or knowing the whole story. Now she was the one who needed to apologize, but would Josh even consider an apology from her? Would she even consider giving him one?

Chapter 9

Josh opened the door of Paul and Carol's house and glared at Adam. "When did you get back into town?"

"Last night."

"I guess you know you've caused problems for me and hurt some innocent "people by posting that video on Facebook."

Adam shrugged. "We were just having fun." He frowned at Josh. "What's happened to you? You used to be all in for pulling pranks. When you left for Arizona last year to play with that band, I missed having you around so when you showed up in Tulsa last week, I thought it would be like old times."

Josh shook his head. "Not anymore. When we were going to OU, we were kids, playing childish pranks, but that was years ago. Those days are behind us."

Adam squinted at Josh. "Sounds to me like your preacher brother is rubbing off on you."

"Maybe so. I just know that while I was in Arizona, I began to see things differently. I'm not going to be a part of something that hurts other people anymore."

"Then how come you agreed to pull the fake robbery?"

Josh cringed and his face grew warm. "To be honest, I needed some cash. I spent all I had getting back to Oklahoma. I shoved my conscience aside so I could win the bet." He swallowed hard. "I lost all the way around."

Adam's face hardened. He crossed his arms over his chest. "So, you're just going to throw it all away, all we've had together as friends."

Josh took a deep breath, knowing he was making an important decision that might change their friendship forever. "I'm not throwing you away, just the things we used to do, things that hurt people. We can still be friends, but no more pranks."

Adam snorted. "You've turned into a wimp since you've been gone." He threw his hands into the air. "So be it." He walked to his car and got in.

Josh followed him and leaned on the door "Do me a favor and take that video off of Facebook."

"Why should I?"

"Several reasons. First, we're embarrassing Cara and Ralph."

Adam sneered. "Oh, it's Cara now. Something going on between you two?"

Josh shook his head. "No, she won't give me the time of day after our prank and now the video, but it's wrong for us to embarrass her like that. She was an innocent bystander and Ralph is a good man. He works hard for his money. We're lucky he didn't call the cops on us."

"I'll think about it."

Josh reached in and touched his shoulder. "You might want to think hard because someone might file charges against us."

Adam shrugged off his hand. "Just let them try it and see what happens."

Josh sighed. He didn't like the sound of that. Adam often carried grudges against those who challenged him. "Where are you off to now?"

"I'm going back to Tulsa. It's home to

me. Why don't you grab your things and go with me?" He raised his hands in mock surrender. "I'll be a good boy."

Josh shook his head. "I'm staying here for the holidays. I want to spend some time with Paul and Carol. It's been a while since I've been with my family. After that, who knows. I'd like to find a place to settle down, get a job, write some music, and maybe do a gig now and then. It's what I've always planned on doing."

Adam studied Josh for a moment. "I feel like we're parting ways for good." He glared at Josh, a hint of anger lighting his eyes. "You might regret that someday." He cranked the engine and pulled out of the church parking lot, tires squealing.

Josh watched until the car disappeared out of sight. "I think you're right, Adam. We have come to a parting of ways. I don't want to live like we have in the past." He turned to go inside and saw the nativity figures on the lawn. His focus rested on the baby in the manger for a moment. He knew what happened that night in Bethlehem had changed those who witnessed it.

Lord, let me see you this Christmas in such a way that it changes me.

***

Cara stared into the darkness and wished for sleep to come. What a horrendous day it had been. First the video posted on Facebook, then her harsh treatment of Josh when he called her. She had been miserable ever since she realized he didn't make the post. How could she straighten all this out? She knew the simple answer. Apologize to Josh, but she couldn't seem to find the courage to do so. She had treated him badly ever since she stepped into the store that day. And now her pride wouldn't let her ask his forgiveness.

That's where the problem lay. She felt justified in putting him in his place. She couldn't bring herself to make amends with him because he had started this whole ugly situation—him and his fake gun. She wondered how he felt about the situation now. Was he having trouble sleeping or was he at peace now that the video had been taken down? She figured he had something to do with it. For once, he had done the right thing.

And now you must do the right thing.

She pulled the blanket over her head, but she knew she couldn't hide—not from that voice.

Chapter 10

Wednesday, November 30

Josh stepped out onto Paul and Carol's front porch Wednesday morning with his cup of coffee and stared in horror at the scene before him. Toilet tissue hung from every shrub and tree branch then draped from one porch column to the next. The nativity scene on the front lawn lay on its face. The wreath from the door lay on the porch. He swatted at the toilet tissue, anger rising in his throat.

"Pretty childish of you, Adam," he said aloud to the empty yard.

"Talking to your…"

Josh turned to see Paul standing in the doorway, his mouth forming an O shape as he gazed around his yard.

Heat crept up Josh's neck and flamed across his face. "I'm sorry, Paul. This is Adam's handiwork, I'm sure."

Paul came out on the porch, continuing to look around at the mess. "Why would he do this to our house?"

"To get back at me."

"I thought you guys were friends."

"Not anymore, I guess." He sighed. "Yesterday, I told him I was staying here, and I didn't want to join him in anymore pranks."

"Any more pranks? Does that mean you've been involved in the past?"

Josh swallowed the lump in his throat. "In college, we were known as the campus pranksters. We got a lot of attention because of it. We even made extra money pulling pranks for people who wanted to get revenge on someone else." Josh ran his hand through his hair and blinked back hot tears of shame that threatened to fall. "When we arrived in town, we pulled a prank on Ralph at his store. That's how I met Cara. She walked in on our fake robbery."

Sadness filled Paul's eyes. "Oh, Josh."

"I know. It was bad of me to get involved, but at the time, we thought it was funny. Now I know better. After spending the past year in Arizona away from Adam, I realized how mean we had been. Yesterday, I told him I wanted a different kind of life and refused to return to Tulsa with him. I guess it upset him more than I thought."

Paul shook his head and gazed around at the mess in his front yard. "We better get this cleaned up before too many people see it."

The two of them worked on the yard until every bit of tissue had been discarded. Thankfully, not too many cars passed by, although one silver Nissan stopped, and the driver stared. When they finally finished, Paul turned to Josh.

"I'm glad you decided not to do this kind of thing anymore. Not only is it childish and immature, but it's not good for your testimony as a Christian and it's not good for the church image."

"I'm sorry, Paul. I didn't dream he would take it out on you to get back at me."

Paul slipped his arm around Josh's shoulders. "Let's put it behind us. I'm glad you've chosen not to get involved in this kind of meanness anymore. If Adam will do this to someone who has been a friend, then he's not the kind of company you need to keep."

Josh nodded. "You're right."

As they stepped up on the porch, Josh silently prayed that Adam had left town and nothing else would happen.

Chapter 11

Cara slammed on the brakes and stared at the sight of toilet tissue strung from one end of the Freeman yard to the other. Who on earth had pulled this stunt? Going down their street wasn't her usual route to work, but Olivia had called and asked for a ride because of car trouble. She lived three houses down from the Freemans.

As Cara stared at the mess, Josh walked out on the porch. She immediately drove on, but she could tell by the look on his face he was shocked. Looks like someone had paid him back for his own trick. Well, it served him right, but she hated it for Paul and Carol's sake.

She pulled in front of Olivia's house

and honked. Olivia rushed out and climbed into the car.

"Thanks for giving me a ride. My car should be ready this evening."

Cara put the car in reverse and started back the way she had come. "Have you seen the fiasco at the Freeman's?"

Olivia shook her head. "No, what happened."

"See for yourself." She nodded toward the Freeman's yard as she drove by. Now Josh and Paul were both outside, pulling the tissue from every spot where it hung.

"Oh, my goodness." Olivia stared at the mess. "Who would do that to a minister?"

"I have a feeling, whoever it was, did it to Josh, not Paul and Carol."

"That's still pretty low. They can't help what Josh did."

Cara sighed. "I know but it looks as though his robbery stunt has backfired."

"You don't think Ralph had anything to do with it, do you?"

"No, but someone may have acted on his behalf."

They drove on to work, forgetting about the scene at the Freeman house as they discussed holiday decorations for the office.

Olivia's forehead wrinkled in thought. "If I remember right, Sam threw all of the old ones away after Christmas last year,"

"He should be back today. Maybe he'll tell us what he wants us to do,"

Olivia groaned. "So soon?"

"It was only a five-day cruise. They were scheduled to arrive back in port on Monday evening. Today's Wednesday, so yes, I expect him to be in the office today."

Olivia frowned. "Just when I was getting used to having the place to ourselves."

Cara laughed. "Yeah, pandemonium will reign once again."

They arrived to find their boss already at work although he normally didn't arrive early. He stepped out of his office as they walked in.

"I see the building is still standing. You girls did pretty good to keep things going." He looked at Cara and chuckled. "Been involved in any more fake robberies?"

"No and I don't plan to be." She changed the subject. "How was your cruise?"

"Top notch. We had a great time. It was good to get away. Now it's back to work." He started toward his office, then stopped and looked around. "I don't see any Christmas frills around here."

"We didn't know what to do about it," Olivia said. "You didn't leave any instructions and the old ones were thrown out last year."

Cara noticed she was careful not to say he had been the one to throw them out. She pressed her lips together to keep from smiling.

He looked puzzled for a moment. "Well, the two of you go get some things and make this place look like it's the holidays." He handed them a charge card just as Emma walked in. "You go with them," he said to her. "I'll take care of things around here until the three of you get back."

Emma looked surprised but followed them out the door. "Where are we going?"

"Shopping for Christmas decorations." Cara frowned. It wasn't how she wanted to start her day, but it might be better than being in the office with Sam on his first day back.

Olivia tapped Emma on the shoulder. "Guess what we saw on the way here."

Emma grinned. "I can probably guess. I saw someone at Lawton's Supermarket with a shopping cart full of tissue last night. Someone's house got it big time."

"The Freeman's." Cara pulled into a parking space in front of Farmer's Pharmacy.

Emma's mouth fell open. "The minister? But why?"

"Cara thinks they did it because Josh is staying there."

Emma nodded. "Makes sense."

"Who was buying the tissue?" Cara clicked the fob to lock the car doors.

"I didn't know him. I've never seen him before."

A sudden thought occurred to her. Josh's friend, Adam who had posted the video seemed a likely suspect. Josh probably asked him to take the video off Facebook and he did it to get back at Josh. She felt sure he was the one, but she kept the information to herself. She had her own situation to make right and she hadn't been able to drum up the courage to do so.

***

The rest of the week passed without further drama. Sam seemed in a rare mood, complimenting them on their work and the Christmas decorations. He even had lunch delivered twice. The ladies raised their eyebrows at each other in surprise but kept their mouths shut. They didn't want to mess up a good thing. If Sam was happy, everybody was happy.

On Friday, Sam had a dinner party to attend so he announced they would be closing the office early. Cara decided to stop by Shelley's Gifts for a new wreath. The parking area was full, so she parked down the street and walked to the store. The fresh, crisp air felt good on her face after being inside the office all day. She noticed a few snow flurries, their first of the season.

She opened the door to the gift shop and was greeted with the sound of live Christmas music. A crowd had gathered so she couldn't see the musician. She wandered through the store admiring the gift items that Shelley had for sale.

"Hi Cara, good to see you."

Shelley Morrison smiled at her. "Can I help you find something, or did you come for the concert?"

"I'm looking for a wreath. I didn't know you were having a concert."

"The wreaths are back here. Let me show you what I've got." Shelley led the way toward the back of the store.

Cara still couldn't see the musician, but whoever it was, he or she was good. She followed Shelley to the wreath display.

"Look to your heart's content. I'm going to check on the refreshments." Shelley disappeared into the crowd.

The musician finished his rendition of "Jingle Bells" and the crowd applauded. He launched into "Do You Hear What I Hear," and Cara stopped her browsing to listen. She had always loved that melody and the lyrics. Whoever played that guitar had a special touch. Something about the style seemed familiar. Suddenly she knew who the musician was even without seeing him. It had to be Josh.

Her first thought was to get out of the store as fast as possible to avoid another encounter with him, but she couldn't get to the door without wading through the people and disrupting things. Might as well decide on a wreath until she could get out. If she stayed on this side of the store, she could probably get away without him seeing her.

Shelley appeared at her side again. "Did you find a wreath you like?"

She held up the two that appealed to her. "I can't decide between the two. I like both of them."

Shelley laughed. "Want me to choose for you?"

"Yes. I'll be happy with either one of them."

"Okay." Shelley grinned. "Close your eyes and I'll choose one and put it in a bag. You can open it when you get home."

While Shelley ran her credit card, Cara glanced at the crowd. A small space opened between two women, and she could see Josh sitting on a stool playing his guitar. The man looked as handsome in jeans and a sports jacket as he had in slacks at church. He smiled as he played. It was obvious he was in his element with the guitar. At that moment, he looked up and their eyes met in the tiny opening between the two women. They stared at each other for a moment, then Cara looked away.

Shelley handed her the card and a receipt. She stuffed it into her purse and picked up the sack with the wreath inside. At that moment, Josh ended his song and the crowd applauded. She turned to go.

What's your hurry?" Shelley asked. "It's been a long time since you've been in. Stay for refreshments and meet Josh." She grinned. "He's single and he's very easy on the eyes. He's a great guitarist, don't you think?"

Cara offered a lame smile. "I've already met him."

"Hi, Cara."

She stopped at the sound of his voice.

Josh stood behind her, smiling. "Good to see you again."

"Hi." She looked around for Shelley, who had mysteriously disappeared into the throng of people in her little store.

At that moment, two older ladies walked up to Josh and began chattering about how much they loved his music. "We were wondering," one of them said, "if you would play for our church Christmas dinner." They slipped their arms through his.

Josh smiled at them. "What date is that?" he asked as he was led away. He glanced back at Cara and shrugged, disappointment clouding his face.

Cara saw her chance to disappear while he became distracted. She slipped through an opening in the crowd and stepped outside. The temperature had dropped since she had been inside the store. She hurried to her car, placed the wreath on the back seat and climbed in. She shivered. It had been sixty degrees this morning. It now felt like a freezing thirty-two. When she arrived home, she immediately changed into a pair of jeans and a sweater, then headed for the kitchen. She had eaten a light lunch. Her stomach growled with hunger. Opening the pantry door, she peered inside. It looked kind of bare. She sorted through the few boxed and canned items and wrinkled her nose. Nothing appealing here. Not even a can of chili or soup. A quick scan of the fridge revealed the same situation.

She thought about going to get something but hated the idea of getting out in the cold air again. She thought for a moment. *Pizza.* The Pizza House made deliveries. She grabbed the phone book, looked up the number, and called. She ordered a thick crust supreme and gave them her credit card and address.

While she waited for the pizza, she opened the sack with the wreath and smiled. Even though she had liked both in the store, Shelley had guessed which one she favored— the silver and red one. She carried it to the front door and hung it on the hook that lived there for whatever wreath she had hanging there for the season. She shivered and closed the door then turned her attention to the bare tree that still stood in the corner of the room. She had just placed it in the tree stand and fluffed out the branches when the doorbell rang. Her pizza. She rushed to open the door. Josh stood there, a pizza box in his hand. Out on the street, she saw the delivery driver pulling away from the curb.

She frowned. "What are you doing with my pizza?"

He smiled. "I hijacked it from the delivery boy. He was more than willing to let me deliver it for a nice tip." He squinted at her. "Do you mind sharing it with me?"

"Do I have a choice?"

Sadness flickered in his eyes. "Yes. If you'd rather I leave, I will. But I would like to talk to you over this great-smelling pizza."

Something about the sadness in his eyes made her step back. "Come in."

"Thank you." He stepped inside and handed her the pizza.

She carried it to the table and set it down. When she turned around, he was unbuttoning his coat. "I'll hang that in the closet for you."

"Thanks." He looked around. "I see you still haven't decorated your tree. The offer to help is still good."

She faced him. "Look, let's get one thing straight. I'll share the pizza with you, and we can talk while we eat, but then you leave. Okay?"

He nodded. "Okay."

She pointed to the sofa. "Have a seat. I'll dish up the pizza and we can eat in here."

In the kitchen, she grabbed two plates from the cabinet and two sodas from the fridge. She dished up the pizza, two slices for herself and four for him, and carried everything to the living room. She stopped in the doorway. Josh was squatted in front of the fireplace placing logs on the grate. For a moment, she resented him making himself at home in her house, but then it would be nice to have a fire tonight.

He stood and saw her in the doorway. "I noticed you had wood and thought you might like a fire on a cold night like this."

"It will feel good." She set the plates and drinks on the coffee table and rearranged the books and magazines to make room for them to eat. She pointed at the plate with four pieces. "That one is yours."

He sat in front of the plate, and she sat on the floor across from him. "Would you like to say grace?"

He shook his head. "It's been a while for me and I'm just now getting back into the prayer thing. Do you mind?"

"Okay." She bowed her head, said a short grace, and looked up to find him watching her. "Did you even bow your head?"

His face reddened. "I'm sorry. I was distracted by you sitting there. I know it sounds like a pick-up line, but you really are an attractive woman."

Cara blushed. No one had said anything like that to her since …

The thought of Brandt annoyed her. She shoved his memory away.

Josh rubbed his chin. "Do you think we should say grace again since I was so irreverent?"

She wondered if he was serious, but then noticed he tried to hold back a smile. "No, I guess not." She took a bite of pizza. "Yum, I'm glad I decided to order in. This is exactly what I'm hungry for."

He took a bite. "It is delicious." He laid his piece on the plate and took a swig of soda. "I'm surprised though. I figured you to be someone who cooks for herself all the time."

"Why would you think that?"

He shrugged. "Well, your mother is an excellent cook, and you made that delicious broccoli salad for Thanksgiving dinner. Guess

I just thought, 'like mother, like daughter.'"

She laughed. "Trust me, Mother taught me to cook, but after working all day, sometimes I just want to come home and chill and let someone else do the cooking."

"I see."

They ate in silence for a moment then she asked, "How did you know where I live?"

He grinned self-consciously. "I asked Shelley. She didn't want to tell me at first, but I told her we already knew each other, and we had something important to discuss."

"You kind of exaggerated the "'already knowing each other,'" didn't you? That's not really the truth."

"But we have spent some time together. We had Thanksgiving dinner at your parent's house. We set up the nativity at the church. Then there is the incident at Ralph's."

Displeasure trickled over her. "You call holding a gun on me the same as spending time with me?"

His face turned red again. "What can I do to make that up to you? I'm so ashamed of that day. I don't know why I let Adam talk me into that. And I'm so sorry about the video. If I had known Adam intended posting it, I would have stopped him."

"So, it was your friend."

"I'm not so sure I can call him a friend anymore."

"Is he the toilet tissue culprit too?"

He looked surprised. "You know about that?"

"Yes, one of the women I work with lives down the street from Paul and Carol. I picked her up for work that morning."

Josh shook his head. "I wish there was something I could do to make up for all this to you and to my brother."

For a moment, Cara enjoyed watching him squirm and eat crow, but then she heard the voice again.

You need to do the right thing.

But Lord, he's the one who started this.

You still need to do the right thing.

Cara sipped her soda and watched him over the top of the can. He did seem remorseful about the incident, and she had been extremely ugly to him ever since.

He's done his part. Are you going to let this grudge continue?

She sighed. "There's something I need to say to you."

He looked up from the slice of pizza he bit into and laid it down. He took a deep breath and appeared to be bracing himself for what she had to say. Had she been that bad to him?

No need to answer that, Lord. I know the answer.

"I apologize for talking to you the way I did when you called me at the office. I thought you posted the video, and I was very angry. I said some things I shouldn't have. I'm sorry." She looked down at the pizza crust on her plate. "In fact, I've been pretty mean to you ever since we met."

His hand closed over hers and she flinched, not sure how she felt about his touch. When she glanced up, he gazed at her as if she had just handed him a million dollars.

"Thank you, Cara. You don't know what it means to hear you say that but if you hadn't, I would still want to be your friend. Although you were certainly justified in anything you said after all that happened." He let go of her hand and took a drink of his soda. "I'm so sorry you were the victim of a thoughtless prank. Trust me when I tell you that I will never do anything like that to you, or anyone else, ever again."

For the first time since she walked into Ralph's and saw him holding the plastic gun, she relaxed in his company. A sense of peace moved over her like a gentle breeze whispering through trees.

He finished his soda and stood. "Thank you for sharing your pizza with me. I guess it's time for me to go."

Suddenly, she didn't want him to leave. She smiled at him. "You're not getting off that easy. We still have a tree to decorate."

His face lit up like a giant light bulb. "Are you serious? You really want me to stay?"

She studied him for a moment. "I think so."

"Thank you." He walked over to the tree and then turned back to her. "Your friendship is like an early Christmas gift."

"Well, it is the season for giving although I would have thought my friendship would be an unlikely gift after the way I've treated you."

They spent the next hour stringing lights on the tree, then Cara plugged it in. The room glowed with multicolored lights.

"Looks good," Josh said. "Reminds me of the trees we had when Paul and I were kids. We always had multicolored lights."

Cara admired the tree. It did look good. Even though she had some misgivings about

Christmas, she loved all the traditions that went along with the season.

She glanced at Josh. He looked like a different person than the one she had seen the day before Thanksgiving. And he was so good-looking she felt like curling up on the sofa and spending the evening talking and enjoying his company, but she didn't. Too soon to let herself relax that much, but she could be a good hostess.

"Would you like a cup of hot chocolate or some hot tea?"

Josh looked up from the box of ornaments he sorted through. "That sounds great. Hot chocolate please. I'm not much of a tea man."

She laughed. "Chocolate it is." She went to the kitchen and rummaged through the pantry for some mix but came up with an empty box. Okay, that meant she would need to make it from scratch which took some time, but she liked it better. She retrieved the ingredients and began mixing them into a pan. A slight noise caused her to look up from her stirring.

Josh stood in the doorway, watching her, a smile lighting his face. "I assume we're having the real thing tonight."

"My mom doesn't believe in the instant mixes. She always makes it from scratch. This is her recipe and mine. Is that okay?"

Josh rubbed his hands together. "Looking forward to it. It's more than okay. Makes me feel special. I haven't had hot chocolate made the old-fashioned way since I left home."

"How long has that been?"

"Ten years."

"You haven't been back to see your parents in ten years?"

Sadness rippled across his countenance. "Our parents died ten years ago within a few months of each other. My mom went first and five months later, dad joined her.

"I'm sorry about your parents. I didn't know."

Cara turned off the burner beneath the pan then went to the cabinet for mugs. She started to reach for the everyday ones but noticed the holiday cups on the top shelf. She stretched but couldn't quite reach them. Oh well, the others would do.

Josh was beside her in an instant reaching over her head to get two of the festive mugs from the top shelf. "Is this what you are trying to reach?"

"Yes, thank you." She took the mugs and returned to the stove where she filled them with the steaming chocolate. She handed him one.

He took a sip and closed his eyes. "Just like I remember." He chuckled. "I can't wait to tell Paul that you make hot chocolate just like our mom did."

She suddenly felt self-conscious knowing Josh would be telling Paul about their evening together. Most people knew she hadn't dated or spent time with a man since Brandt's disappearance. She wasn't sure what people would think. More to the point, she wasn't sure how she felt about it...yet.

"Cara."

His voice jolted her back to the present. "Sorry, just thinking about us having hot chocolate after everything that's happened." Their eyes met and she couldn't look away. She had to admit he seemed even more handsome than Brandt and she had thought no one better looking at the time.

He spoke softly, his eyes still locked on hers. "It is quite a change for us, isn't it?"

She nodded and glanced away, the atmosphere in the room getting a bit too intimate for her.

She heard him clear his throat and looked up.

"Let's go take a look at the ornaments." He motioned toward the living room.

He didn't have to ask her twice. She followed him and set her mug on the coffee table. She grabbed a couple of ornaments and placed them on the tree. He followed suit. They worked quietly for a few minutes then he stepped back, picked up his mug and took a drink.

"It's looking better all the time."

Cara picked up her own cup. "Yes, I like it. I'm glad I bought new ornaments and lights. It needed a change."

"Kind of like us."

Her mouth went dry, and her stomach fluttered. This was getting more personal than she wanted it to. With the glow from the tree and the fireplace, sharing a meal and now hot chocolate, the atmosphere in the room had taken on a romantic feeling.

She collected their mugs and carried them to the kitchen. When she returned, he had taken his coat out of the closet. He buttoned it and then pulled on his gloves. He checked his pockets.

"I must have left my scarf at Shelley's

shop." He walked to the door. "Thank you for letting me share your pizza and tree trimming. I've enjoyed it."

She followed him to the door. "Thanks for your help."

He looked at her for a moment, his eyes gentle. "You're welcome." He opened the door and stepped out on the porch.

"Goodnight."

"Goodnight, Cara. Thanks for the best evening I've had in a long time." He turned toward the street.

She closed the door and collapsed on the sofa, feeling a bit lightheaded. What had just happened? She had spent the entire evening with a man she couldn't stand a few days ago. Once they began talking, she had relaxed and enjoyed herself. That had been the most surprising part.

It makes a difference when you do the right thing.

It did. She could feel it. It was that something else she thought she felt that concerned her. She had given her heart away once and had it broken. She wouldn't let that happen again. But the friendship tonight had been nice for a change.

Cara cleaned up the boxes and paper

littering the floor, turned out the lights, and unplugged the tree. Pajamas and a warm bed sounded good. As she headed toward her bedroom, her cell phone rang.

"Hello."

"Cara, this is Paul Freeman. I'm sorry to bother you, but we're concerned about Josh. He played his guitar at Shelley's Gifts this afternoon, but he hasn't come home. When I called her, she said he had asked for your address."

"Yes, he was here earlier." She glanced at the time on her phone. "He left about fifteen minutes ago."

"I better go look for him. It's too cold to be out walking in this weather."

A feeling of alarm shot through her, and her heart started to race. She had closed the door so quickly when he left that she didn't notice there wasn't a car parked in the drive.

"Paul, are you telling me he is out walking somewhere in this freezing weather?"

"I'm afraid so, Cara. He doesn't have a car, but he said he would hitch a ride if he needed to."

"I'm so sorry. I didn't realize…"

"It's okay, Cara. Thank you." Paul disconnected the call.

Paul and Carol must think her a poor friend. She had been in such a hurry to close the door she hadn't even bothered to see him off properly. That meant he had not only walked over here earlier, but he would have to walk all the way home. Redwood was a small town, but the Freemans lived across on the other side. It would be quite a trek in thirty-degree weather.

She needed to help Paul find him. She grabbed her coat and gloves from the closet, pulled them on then picked up her cell and headed out to the garage. She gave the engine a moment to warm up then backed down the drive and out into the street. She turned up the heater and warm air poured through the vents.

She drove slowly, glancing from side to side as she went. When she reached the town square and Shelley's Gifts, she stopped.

"Oh Josh, where are you? Why didn't I watch to see which direction he took? More to the point, why didn't I notice he didn't have a car?"

Without warning, a tear trickled down her cheek. She brushed it away and moved on. As she passed the bank, she noticed the temperature read twenty-nine degrees. Sleet hit the windshield as she turned onto a side street into a residential neighborhood. Josh was somewhere out in this weather and she was to blame.

She turned on the wipers and made another turn. Up ahead, she saw a figure bent over against the wind and sleet. She honked her horn, but he kept walking. She pulled up even with him and honked again. He stopped and turned around.

She rolled down the window. "Josh, get in."

He opened the door and climbed inside. She wanted to cry at the sight of ice particles stuck in his hair and eyebrows.

"What are you doing out here?" He rubbed his hands together.

"Paul called me. He's worried about you." Without warning, tears filled her eyes. "Oh Josh, why didn't you tell me you didn't have a car. I'm so sorry."

"I didn't want to bother you. You've had enough trouble because of me. No sense adding anything else to it. But boy am I glad you came along. It's freezing out there."

She picked up her cell. "We better call Paul and let him know."

When Paul answered, she told him she had found Josh and would bring him home.

They arrived at the house at the same time. She followed Paul and Carol into their driveway. They both jumped out of their car and ran to Josh, pulling his door open.

Josh stepped out of the car and Paul pulled him into a hug. "Josh, you should have called me from Cara's house. I would have come for you. Let's get you inside and get some hot liquid into you."

Paul turned to Cara. "You're welcome to come in if you'd like to."

She shook her head. "It's late. We all need to get in bed soon."

Josh said something to Paul that she couldn't hear then he and Carol went inside. Josh sat down in the car again. He reached over and took Cara's hand. "It means a lot to me that you came out looking for me. Thank you."

Cara brushed at her tears with her free hand. "I'm so sorry you had to walk in this weather, Josh. Please forgive me."

"There's nothing to forgive. How could you know I didn't have a car?" He squeezed her hand. "I better get inside and get warm. I feel like a big chunk of ice." He slid out of the seat and closed the door.

Cara watched him walk to the door

where he turned and waved before he stepped inside. She waved back and then headed home.

Later, as she lay in bed, she thought about something. Josh had walked to her house from Shelley's Gifts and then started walking home in freezing weather just so he could be with her. Brandt had never done anything like that. In fact, no man ever had. Josh was the exception. That made him …special.

Chapter 12

Sunday, December 4

Cara didn't hear from Josh on Saturday, and she didn't attempt to call him either. She wasn't sure about what was happening between them, and she wasn't sure if she wanted anything to come of it. Her heart still remembered Brandt's behavior and kept putting up a defense.

On Sunday morning as she dressed for church, she realized he would be there. A little shiver of excitement surprised her. She didn't know how he would act toward her but if he didn't point a plastic gun at her, she would be okay with seeing him.

She laughed at her reflection in the mirror and realized she had gotten past the fake robbery. She had forgiven him.

As she pulled into the parking lot, she noticed a group of people standing out front, which seemed kind of odd given that the temperature hovered in the thirties. She got out of her car and walked over to them. When she got closer, it was clear there had been some vandalism at the church.

Cara gasped when she saw the nativity figures had been sprayed with red paint. She looked around for Josh and saw him talking to Paul near the front door. He noticed her about the same time and gave a small wave, but he didn't call her over, so she stayed with the crowd. When her parents arrived, she went inside with them.

Soon afterwards, Paul and the others came inside. He spoke to the choir director in quiet tones and then stepped to the front.

"As you all noticed, we had some trouble last night but we're not going to let that stop us from having worship service this morning. I know you're upset, hurt, angry. Open your hearts to God and allow him to fill you with forgiveness for the one who committed this malicious act. Allow God's Spirit to bring you peace." He nodded at the choir director and the choir broke into song with "Great is Thy Faithfulness."

Cara looked around for Josh, but he wasn't sitting with the rest of the orchestra, and she didn't see him in the audience that sat in front of her or to either side. She wondered if he had stayed outside.

Paul spoke about the angel's message of peace on earth, goodwill to men. "In spite of what has happened to the nativity outside, we must pursue peace and goodwill with those around us."

Distracted and not knowing the whereabouts of Josh, Cara only heard part of what Paul said until he mentioned that God loved us so much, he sent his Son Jesus to show us the way by his death on the cross.

"We are to love like Christ did. No matter what comes our way, He's got our best interest at heart."

Cara cringed. The familiar feeling of resentment returned. If He loved her that much, why did he allow Brandt to abandon her? He could have stopped him. Why didn't he? Her thoughts made her uncomfortable here in the church. Relief swept over her when the service ended. As she stood, she looked around the building for Josh, but she didn't see him anywhere.

Her dad tapped her on the shoulder. "Hey, sweetheart, how about going to lunch with us? We're headed to Riley's for burgers and fries."

"I guess so." She kept looking around for Josh.

"Is something wrong?" her mother asked. "You seem distracted this morning."

She shook her head. "Just wondering about the vandalism and who would do such a thing." Even as she said it, she knew the guilty party had to be Adam.

As they walked out the front door, Paul stopped her. "Cara, Josh gave me a message for you." He handed her a folded piece of paper.

"Is he okay?"

Paul nodded. "Yes, I think so."

She waited until she was inside her car to unfold the note.

Cara,

I'm sorry we didn't get a chance to talk this morning. As you can see, Adam is still trying to get even with me. I'm sure he is the one who spray painted the nativity scene. I'm

going to find him and see if I can talk some sense into him. I'm not sure if he's still in town so it may mean I have to leave Redwood for a while. Talk to you soon.
Love, Josh.

P.S. Friday night was a special time for me. I hope it was for you too.

Hot tears stung her eyes. This man had walked through freezing weather to spend time with her. He had forgiven her for being rude and saying cruel things to him. He had helped her decorate her tree. He appreciated the simplest of things like a cup of homemade hot chocolate. What had she done for him? What had she done to deserve such kindness?

It's called grace, my child.

Chapter 13

Saturday, December 10

The next week passed without a word from Josh. Cara thought about him every day. She wanted to call Paul and Carol to ask if they had heard anything but restrained herself. They weren't in a serious relationship and had only met the day before Thanksgiving.

On Saturday morning, she found herself wandering from room to room as if searching for something. She ended up in the kitchen where she pulled out her recipe for Christmas cookies and mixed up a batch. She would take some to the office on Monday, keep some here to munch on, and save a dozen for Josh. When the cookies were all baked, she found herself wandering the house again.

I've got to get out of here for a while. She dressed in warm clothes and drove to Shelley's Gifts to do some shopping. As she browsed through the merchandise, her mind kept returning to the possibility that Josh might not come back.

She stopped in front of a display of candles. Shelley had arranged them in front of a mirror to highlight the products. Cara looked through the various scents and picked up a large decorative candle. As she did, she glimpsed someone in the mirror. *Brandt stood right behind her.* Her heart started pounding as she jerked around. She stared at him in disbelief.

Her voice squeaked when she spoke. "What are you doing here?"

He smiled. "I came to see you, Cara." He reached out to her, and she jerked back as though she might be burned.

He frowned. "What's wrong? Aren't you glad to see me?"

Her pulse raced and she felt as though she might faint. "After what you did to me? I never want to see you again, Brandt Peters. Get away from me."

"You mean because I decided not to get married? Is that what you're referring to?"

Hot tears stung her eyes. "You abandoned me on our wedding day."

"Is that what you think I did?"

"I know that's what you did. We had a church full of people waiting to hear us say our vows and you never showed."

He chuckled and she wanted to slap him, but she remembered where they were and controlled herself. She scanned the store to see if anyone had noticed him, but everyone seemed preoccupied with their shopping. She had to get out of here. She moved to step around him, but he blocked her escape.

He leaned closer to her. "Let's go somewhere so we can be alone and talk without anyone else around."

She glared at him. "I'm not going anywhere with you so get out of my way." She tried to sidestep him, but he moved into her path again.

"Go away, Brandt. I'm not interested in talking to you. I hoped never to see you again."

He laughed and held out his arms. "Surprise, here I am."

"Get out of my way."

He shook his head. "No can do, Cara. I came to see you and that's just what I intend to do."

"Over my dead body."

His smile disappeared. "I would hate for it to come to that, but …" He didn't finish the sentence, just stared at her, his face tightening into a hard glare.

For the first time, she felt scared. This wasn't the Brandt she had known and almost married. There was something eerie about him. Just then Shelley approached them.

"Hi Cara, what can I help you with today?"

Relief spread through her. She handed Shelley the candle she had been holding. "I'll take this. Can you wrap it for me?"

"Sure thing, Cara." At that moment, Shelley realized who stood beside her and she frowned.

"Hello, Brandt. I didn't know you were back in town."

He gave her his most charming smile. "Why yes, I came to see my folks and my best girl." He glanced at Cara. His eyes challenged her to contradict him.

Shelley looked at Cara. "I'll get this wrapped for you. Are you going to wait for it?"

Cara nodded. "If you don't mind."

"I'll get right on it." She gave Brandt another scathing glare and walked toward the back of the store.

Cara took the chance and followed Shelley. She could feel Brandt's eyes on her, but she kept walking. When they reached the counter in the back of the store, Shelley stepped around to the other side and looked at Cara.

"Is anything wrong?"

Cara nodded. "I need to get away from him. Can you call my dad?"

Shelley stepped over to the computer where her cell lay. She didn't pick it up, just opened the call screen. "What's the number?"

For a minute, Cara couldn't think. She closed her eyes and recited the number as it came to her. Shelley keyed it in, and a screen appeared. She typed a text then turned it around so Cara could read it.

Mr. Phillips, can you come to Shelley's Gifts downtown. Cara needs you right away.

Immediately he sent a response.

I'll be right there.

Shelley nodded at Cara and then picked up the candle and began gift wrapping it. "So, are you finished with your shopping, Cara?"

Cara took a deep breath, grateful for Shelley's attempt at acting normal. "No, I'm just getting started. In fact, this is my first gift to buy." She lowered her voice. "Is he still in here."

Shelley nodded, then continued their conversation. "I have lots of nice gift items I can show you."

"Thank you."

Shelley handed the gift-wrapped candle to Cara. "Would you like me to show you some things?"

Before she could respond, Brandt appeared beside her. "We need to go, Cara. if we're going to have lunch." He rubbed his stomach. "I'm getting hungry."

Fury swept over her, but she kept her composure. How dare he show up and interfere in her life after the way he had treated her. "Why don't you go ahead and get something to eat. I'm not really hungry and I have more shopping to do."

He glared at her and shook his head. "No, I'll wait. We're going together."

Cara felt tiny fingers of fear crawling up her spine as she realized he meant business. He wasn't going to leave her alone. "Suit yourself." She turned away from him.

Brandt grabbed her arm. "I think we should go now."

In the distance, Cara heard the bell over the door ring and out of the corner of her eye, she saw her dad approaching. When he noticed Brandt, shock leaped into his eyes but quickly turned to rage.

"Peters, take your hand off my daughter." The authority in his voice would have made even the strongest man run.

Brandt let go of Cara's arm. "Hey, Mr. Phillips. Good to see you." He extended his hand, but Don Phillips ignored the outstretched hand and marched up to him. They were so close, their noses almost touched.

"I don't know what you're doing here but get away from Cara. She doesn't want to see you. You've done enough damage around here already."

Brandt tried to laugh, but it came out sounding more like a hiccup. "I can explain everything, Mr. Phillips."

"I'm not interested in hearing your explanation and neither is my daughter. You've got exactly one minute to get out of this store before I call the sheriff."

Brandt turned on his heel and hurried toward the entrance. He jerked it open and disappeared.

Her dad reached out for her, and Cara fell into his arms sobbing and trembling. She hadn't realized just how scared she was until she felt her dad's protective arms around her.

She suddenly remembered the other customers in the store and pulled away with a shaky breath, heat rising into her cheeks. Great, she'd be the talk of the town...again.

Don looked at Shelley. "Is there someplace we can go until Cara composes herself?"

Shelley nodded. "Of course, follow

me." Shelley showed them to a room in the back with a table and some chairs. Her dad led her to the sofa in the corner and sat beside her.

"Where did he come from?"

Cara shook her head and wiped at her tears with a trembling hand. "I don't know. One minute I'm shopping and the next minute he's standing behind me." She went on to tell her dad about their conversation. As she talked her dad's face grew more somber.

"I don't like the sound of this, Cara." His eyes narrowed. "I don't mean to frighten you, but he could cause trouble. It sounds as though he may have some emotional problems we didn't know about before."

"What are we going to do?"

"First of all, we're going to see Sheriff Willis and alert him to Brandt's presence in town and ask him what steps to take." He reached over and took Cara's hand in his. "Don't worry, I'm not going to let him hurt you again."

Shelley appeared with a cup. "Here, drink this. It's chamomile tea. It will help you feel better."

Cara smiled weakly. "Thank you. I don't know what I would have done without your help."

"Do you remember Gerald Fortenberry, the dentist that used to be in town? I had the same problem with him. Thank goodness, someone helped me too." She turned to Don Phillips. "I overheard you say you're going to see Ed Willis. The sooner the better. That's the best step you can take to head off trouble."

Cara sipped the tea and slowly began to feel better. When she felt like she could stand on her own two feet she looked at her dad and nodded. "I'm ready."

They stepped out into the cold December air. Her dad led her to his pickup parked across the street. When they were settled inside, he turned to her. "I think you should stay at our house tonight. From what you've told me, Brandt is unpredictable. He doesn't sound like himself." He exhaled sharply. "Although anyone who would abandon another person, he's supposed to love, has a problem to begin with.

Cara sighed. How on earth had she not seen the real Brandt before?

Chapter 14

Sunday, December 11

The first person Cara saw the next morning was Josh standing on the church steps. As soon as he saw her, he came jogging across the parking lot and hugged her. A warm feeling seeped into her spirit. She had spent a sleepless night at her parent's house because of the incident with Brandt. She realized she had missed Josh which surprised her immensely.

"When did you get back?" She stepped back from his hug. Several people had noticed them including her parents who looked puzzled at their greeting.

"Late last night. It was after one, so I didn't want to call and wake you. I knew you would be at church this morning, so I forced myself to wait and see you here." He looked down at Cara, his eyes tender and kind. "It wasn't easy to wait. I missed you. After last Friday night, I haven't been able to think of anything or anyone but you."

She blushed. "It's good to see you too." She wasn't ready to admit she had missed him, or the fact that he too had been on her mind quite a bit the past week. Guarding her heart came first, especially after seeing Brandt yesterday.

"You really mean that?"

She nodded. "Yes."

He smiled. "That's good to hear." He glanced at his watch. "We better get inside. It's time for service to start."

They walked across the parking lot together and he opened the door. When they stepped inside, he leaned down and whispered in her ear. "I'll see you after service."

Before she had time to respond, he walked toward the orchestra platform and took his place. She found her family in their usual seats, but before she reached them, she spotted Brandt's parents. Her heart skipped and she shivered. Was he with them? She scanned the area where they were sitting but didn't see any sign of Brandt. There were no available seats beside her parents' so she slipped into the empty chair behind them.

The music calmed her, and she relaxed knowing her dad sat right in front of her if she needed him. He had always been there for her. She could rely on him in any situation. Just like yesterday. All she had to do was call him and he came to her aid without question.

So will I if you ask me.

Cara startled as if someone had spoken out loud. She realized God spoke to her heart. Then why didn't he come to her aid when Brandt left her?

I was right there all the time waiting for you to invite me into the situation.

She cringed. You knew I needed help.

And you knew where to find me. You allowed your pain to blind you to my love. You ignored all the warning signs about him.

She cringed again. There had been warning signs, but she chose to ignore them because she thought things would be different once they married. Her brother had told her Brandt wasn't trustworthy, but he wouldn't tell her how he knew that. Her dad had asked her repeatedly if she was sure he was the right one. He must have known something too.

Then why didn't they tell her what they knew? Then there was the time she found a stash of money in his glove compartment.

"What is all this money doing in here?" she had asked.

Brandt had laughed and shrugged it off. "It belongs to one of my friends. He won it playing poker and didn't want his wife to know about it. He asked me to hold on to it for him."

She hadn't questioned him because she had believed him. A few days later, he showed her a new cell phone he had purchased. Now she wondered if he had been lying. There must have been two or three thousand dollars in that envelope. If so, what was he doing with that much cash? And where did it come from?

"Do you really think we can afford that so close to the wedding?" she had asked.

For a second, he looked angry, but then he laughed. "Don't worry, I'm on the monthly payment plan."

Tears sprang to her eyes. She had been blind, or maybe she chose to be blind because she thought there was no other man like Brandt Peters. He was handsome, charming, smart, popular… and she felt lucky to be the one he had chosen.

Oh God, I was so blind. Forgive me.

As she spoke the words, a picture of her dad standing in Shelley's store yesterday flashed before her. He had held out his open arms to her and she had run into them. He had held her close while she sobbed.

My arms are open. All you have to do is run into them.

She bowed her head, and, in her mind and heart, she went running into God's open arms. Tears rolled down her face as his peace and comfort filled her to overflowing.

If someone had asked her what the sermon was about or what songs they had sung, she couldn't have told them, but she knew what had happened to her. She had finally given her pain, bitterness, and resentment to God. She had run into his arms and allowed him to take control of her life.

Josh appeared at her side as soon as the service ended, his eyes full of concern. "What was going on with you during the service? Your mind seemed to be somewhere else."

She smiled. "I needed to get some things straightened out."

He studied her for a moment. "So did you get everything straightened out?"

"Yes, I think I did."

He looked puzzled but didn't question her further. "Have plans for lunch?"

"No."

Her mother stepped over to them. "Josh, how about coming to our house? Cara's dad smoked a brisket last night. We have plenty."

He glanced at Cara. She nodded. "Thank you, that sounds great."

When they were alone in her car, she turned to Josh "So, what about Adam? Did you find him?"

He shook his head. "No, I've looked everywhere for him. He seems to have disappeared. I even rented a car and drove to Oklahoma and talked to our friends, went to all our old hangouts, even watched the house of a girl he dates, but nothing." He shrugged. "Maybe it's over and there won't be any more incidents."

As she drove toward her parent's house, they discussed the past week, but she didn't tell him about Brandt. Hopefully, there wouldn't be any more incidents with him either.

Chapter 15

Monday, December 12th

The next morning, Cara scrolled through Facebook sipping her coffee. Nothing interest- ing showed up until Josh's face appeared on the screen holding the fake gun. She glanced to see who had posted it and saw Adam's name. Wherever he was, he was up to his old tricks. She called Josh.

"Good morning, Sunshine," he said.

"The video is back on Facebook."

"You've got to be kidding. Give me a second." Silence echoed on the other end for a moment. "I can't believe he's doing this to me. We were friends for so many years. I thought he would respect my feelings, but I guess not."

"Does this mean he's somewhere around here?"

"Not necessarily. He could post from anywhere in the world."

"Is it too much to hope he'll take it down soon?"

"We can always hope but knowing Adam, it isn't too likely. I'm sorry. One good thing is you're not in it for long and it's not a close-up."

Cara heard him exhale in frustration. "What would happen if we just ignored it and didn't respond?"

"He might eventually pull it. Maybe that's what we need to do—ignore it, and see if he stops. Can I call you back later? I need to talk to Paul and let him know what's going on so he can be prepared for any fallout."

"Of course. I need to get to work anyway."

As she pulled away from her house, she wondered if maybe she should go by and let Ralph know the video was up again. She turned in the direction of the Grab It 'N Go and gasped as she pulled into the parking lot. Ralph's Christmas tree lay on its side, crushed flat. Someone must have run over it. As she stepped from her car, Ralph came out and started across the lot picking up bits of tree and broken lights along the way. When he reached the tree, he stopped, shaking his head.

Cara hurried over to him. "Ralph, I'm sorry about your tree. Some people just don't respect other people's property."

"I should have known it wouldn't make it the whole season. I just hoped…" He shook his head again and his eyes glistened with unshed tears.

"Is there anything I can do?"

"Thanks, Cara, but I'll get my son to help me clean it up." He looked toward the store. "My wife is in there if you need to make a purchase."

"I hate to bring more bad news, but I didn't want you to hear it from someone else who might give you a hard time about it."

"If you mean the video, I already know about it. My son told me earlier."

The sadness on his face made her want to hug him. "You're really getting the full treatment from whoever is doing all this."

"I think it's the same person doing it."

She nodded. "I think you're right. You know Josh went looking for him last week, even went to Oklahoma."

Ralph frowned at her. "By Josh, do you

mean the fake gunman?"

"Yes."

"Y'all friends now?"

Uh-oh. She hadn't thought about how that might look to Ralph. "Yes, you could say that. We had a long talk and he apologized. I was mad for a while, but I've forgiven him."

Ralph shrugged. "Well, he may be okay, but that friend of his is a troublemaker big time."

Cara nodded. "I agree." She looked at her watch. "I better get to work before Sam docks my pay."

The morning passed without incident. At noon, the office door opened, and Josh walked in. Her pulse quickened at the sight of his handsome face.

He walked to her desk and smiled. "How about lunch? I've got Paul's car and we can go anywhere you would like."

"Okay, let me log off my computer and I'll be ready."

As they walked toward Paul's car, he took her hand in his. Two weeks ago, she would have pulled away from him, but it was him who pulled away when they reached the car—but only because he opened the door for her.

When he slid in on the other side, her heart skipped. This was their first time to go anywhere together, and it felt like a date. Was it a date? Did he feel that way about it? She looked over at him.

He smiled as he pulled out into the street. "Other than the Friday I hijacked your pizza; this is our first date."

Her heart hammered inside her chest. Wow. They were on the same page, thinking the same thoughts. What did that mean? She didn't have time to consider it further.

Without warning, a sudden jolt pitched her body forward, straining against the seat belt. She jerked around and looked at Josh. His hand was on her shoulder, bracing her.

"Are you okay?"

"I'm fine. What happened?" She strained to see out the rear window.

"Some nut rear-ended us."

Just then the other car whipped around them and raced off but not before Cara had a chance to see the driver's face. *Brandt Peters.*

Chapter 16

Josh climbed out of Paul's car and walked around to the back of the vehicle. The rear bumper had taken quite a beating. He inspected the damage and felt sick to his stomach. Paul had loaned him the car in good faith that he would take care of it and now this. He pulled out his cell and dialed 9-1-1 to report the hit and run. Then he called Paul.

"I have some bad news."

"What is it, Josh? Are you okay?"

"We're fine, but we have been involved in a hit and run accident."

"We? Is Cara with you? Is she okay?"

"Yes, she's fine too, but your car has

some damage."

"As long as you're both okay, that's what counts. You'll find the insurance information in the glove compartment. Did you call the sheriff's office?"

"Yes, they're on their way. I'm really sorry, Paul. It seems like everything I touch goes bad."

"It wasn't your fault. Don't worry about it, I'm covered. I'm just happy you and Cara are okay. I'll call my mechanic, have it towed, and arrange for a rental car. Just hang tight until it gets there. Call me if you have any problems. I'll see you when you get back. And Josh, don't let it get you down. It can happen to anyone."

He disconnected the call. It was just like Paul not to think of himself first. Anyone else might have been more worried about the car and what it would cost to get it repaired, but Paul always thought of others. He looked at Cara sat in the car, talking to someone on the phone. He walked over and opened the door on her side.

"Dad, I'll talk to you later." She disconnected and looked at Josh. "I think there's something you should know before the sheriff arrives."

"I know who hit us, and I know why."

Josh's eyes widened. "What do you mean, you know why he hit us?"

For the next few minutes, Cara gave Josh the condensed version about Brandt abandoning her at the altar and showing up in town on Saturday. He listened without comment, but anger rose inside him as he heard how Brandt had treated her.

He reached for her hand. "I'm so sorry you had to go through that. I wish you had told me sooner." He shrugged. "But we didn't get started off on the best of terms, did we."

Sheriff Ed Willis walked up to the car. For the next few minutes, they answered questions about the accident, then Cara gave him the news.

"Mr. Willis, it was Brandt Peters that hit us."

The sheriff pushed his Stetson back on his head. "Why didn't you say so? I've been looking for that young man. I've been checking on him since you and your dad came in on Saturday. There's a warrant out for him in South Texas. Seems he was involved in a robbery and some smuggling down there." His face took on a grim appearance. "Keep your eyes open. If you see him or suspect you know where he is, call me immediately." He shook his head. "Be careful, Cara. I believe he could be dangerous where you're concerned." He inclined his head toward Josh. "He's probably not too happy to see you with another man."

Josh glanced at Cara and saw panic in her eyes. He moved closer to her and could feel the intensity of her fear. She glanced up at him and he slipped his arm around her shoulders. A feeling of protectiveness overcame him and for the first time in his life, he wanted to take care of someone besides himself.

Chapter 17

Tuesday, December 13

Cara's cell rang as she stepped out of the shower.

"Good morning, Sunshine."

She smiled at the sound of Josh's voice. "Hi. What are you doing up so early?"

"I'll pick you up and take you to work this morning. What time do you need to be there?"

She frowned and the old defensive nature rose inside her. She pulled the towel tighter around her. "That's not necessary. I'm perfectly capable of driving myself to work."

Josh chuckled. "I know you are, but I would feel better being with you with that Peters guy running loose."

The defensive feeling softened. "That's sweet of you, Josh, but I'll have my cell with me. If I see him, I'll call for help."

Silence hung between them for a moment before she continued. "I appreciate what you're trying to do, but I don't think it's necessary." Even as she spoke the words, she felt a tingle of fear go down her spine. The Brandt they were talking about wasn't the same man she had once loved.

Josh sighed through the phone. "Can I at least take you to lunch?"

She laughed. "Are you sure you want to try that again after what happened yesterday?"

Josh chuckled. "At least it's not Paul's car."

"Okay, we'll do lunch."

Josh walked into the office promptly at noon. As they walked to the rental car, Cara looked around for any clue that Brandt might be hanging around, but everything seemed normal.

They pulled into the Burger Shack parking area and Josh opened the door for her. As she stepped out of the car, someone called her name. She turned around to see Greg and Haley walking toward them. The four of them entered the building together and found an empty table.

After the waitress took their orders, Greg turned to Cara. "Dad tells me Brandt is causing you grief."

"He told you about the hit and run yesterday?"

Greg nodded. "Yes, and also about Saturday when he cornered you at the gift shop." He frowned and shook his head. "I can't say I'm surprised, but I sure don't like it. It makes me afraid for you little sister."

Cara arched one eyebrow at him. "Why are you not surprised? I know that he wasn't your favorite person when we were engaged, but you would never tell me why."

Greg shrugged. "You weren't ready to hear anything negative about Brandt Peters, but for starters, he was a habitual liar. Didn't you ever catch him lying to you?"

Cara thought for a moment. "There were times when I wondered about things like when I found a bunch of cash in an envelope in his car. He said he was holding it for someone else."

Greg took a deep breath. "So, you didn't

know he was into gambling?"

Shock coursed through Cara. "No, I had no idea." She slowly shook her head. "I wonder what else he was involved in that I didn't know about."

"Not much telling." Greg saluted her with his coffee cup. "I'm just glad you didn't marry him. I couldn't say that to you before because you were in such a state of grief over him disappearing. I know Mom and Dad are glad it didn't work out." He took a sip of his iced tea. "Someone was watching over you whether you knew it or not, little sister and kept you from getting into a dangerous situation." He briefly raised his eyes to the ceiling.

A warmth spread over Cara's body. *Yes, Lord, I guess you were. I'm sorry.*

Josh cleared his throat. "I for one am glad she didn't get into it either."

The three of them looked at him. He stared intently at Cara, concern clouding his face.

Cara felt that warm feeling spread through her again, the same one she had felt when the accident happened, and he had put his arm around her. She smiled at him. "Thank you, Josh."

It was Greg's turn to clear his throat. "I'm glad to see that the two of you have become friends. You got off to a shaky start."

A pained expression crossed Josh's face. "I can't tell you how much I regret that incident." He looked over at Cara. "I'm just glad Cara found it in her heart to forgive me."

The waitress showed up with their orders and conversation came to a halt. When she left, Greg said grace and they began eating. The rest of the meal was light-hearted despite recent events and as they walked out to the car, Josh took her hand in his. Again, she realized she hadn't flinched or pulled away. She was losing some of the fear and defensiveness she had harbored over the past year.

When she arrived back at the office, she sat down at her desk, feeling better than she had in some time. An envelope lay on her desk. Her name was scribbled across the front. She pulled out a single sheet of paper and opened it. The good feeling shattered.

Cara,

We need to talk. I want us to get back together. I know you're seeing someone else, but he doesn't know you or love you like I do. Break it off with him. I'll get in touch with you

later and let you know when and where.
And Cara, if you don't, you'll be sorry.
Brandt

An uncontrollable shudder shook her body as she scanned the threatening words. The sheriff was right. Brandt was dangerous. She reached for her cell and dialed the sheriff's office, her hand shaking so badly, she had to start over twice.

"Sheriff Willis speaking."

"This is Cara Phillips." Her voice shook.

"Cara, what's wrong? Has Peters done something?"

"He left a threatening note on my office desk."

"I'll be right there." He hung up before she could say anything else.

Sam appeared in the doorway from his office. He frowned at her. "Are you okay? You're white as a sheet."

She didn't answer, just held out the note to Sam, who read it and swore under his breath. "Did you call the sheriff?"

Cara nodded. "He's coming."

"Let me know when he gets here." Sam disappeared back inside his office.

Emma walked over. "What's going on?"

Cara handed her the note. Emma's eyes widened and Olivia put a hand over her mouth as she read over Emma's shoulder.

The door opened and Sheriff Willis walked in. His eyes scanned the entire area as he strode toward Cara's desk. "Cara, you, okay?"

She nodded and handed him the note.

He studied it for a minute and looked up. "Did any of you see him put the note on Cara's desk?"

The three of them shook their heads. Sam appeared in his doorway. "Sheriff, I think I know what happened." They all looked at him in surprise.

"After the three of them left for lunch, I was in my office on the phone when I heard the door open. I thought it was either a client or one of them had come back early. I ended my call, but when I came out here, the room was empty."

The sheriff rubbed his chin. "So, he was watching the office and when they all left, he slipped in and left the note on Cara's desk." He looked at Sam. "Evidently, he wasn't afraid to slip in with you in your office."

Sam nodded. "While he and Cara were together, he got to know the office routine pretty well. I guess he knew he had enough time to slip in and out before I came to check on things."

Sheriff Willis folded the note. "Cara, I'm taking this with me. It's proof that he intends harm if you don't do what he asks. If I were you, I would stay at your folk's house for a while until we catch him." He walked to the door. "Be aware of your surroundings at all times. Don't go anywhere alone."

After the sheriff left, Cara tried to focus on work, but she couldn't stop thinking about the note and Brandt's threatening words. They kept playing through her mind like a broken recording. A frightening thought crossed her mind. Brandt might do something to Josh or someone in her family if she didn't agree to meet him.

Chapter 18

That evening after dinner, she told her father everything. "There is only one thing to do. I have to meet with Brandt." She tried to control her voice, but it still shook a bit.

Don Phillips shook his head. "Absolutely not."

"Dad, it's the only way we can be sure of catching him. He's smart and he's sneaky. If I agree to meet him, the sheriff and his deputies can be waiting to arrest him." She sighed wearily. "I want to be done with this thing. I want to move on with my life and not be looking over my shoulder knowing he's out there somewhere."

"It's too dangerous. He might hurt you."

"Not if I have protection."

Her dad shook his head, his lips pressed together in a grim line. She knew it was impossible to change his mind when he had that look on his face. She stood and carried her plate to the sink.

Her mother joined her and reached to turn on the water. "Cara, your dad is worried about you. He's afraid for you." She rinsed off the plate in her hand and placed it in the dishwasher. "I know you want to have a life free of Brandt. I've watched you grieve the past year and suffer because of him, but I agree with your dad. It is too dangerous." Her mother pulled her into a hug. "You're still our baby girl, even if you're a grown woman, and we love you. We couldn't stand it if something happened to you."

Cara planted a kiss on her mother's cheek. "I know." She went back to the table for more dishes. The phone rang in the other room, and she heard her dad's voice as he answered the call. There was silence for a moment before he spoke again.

"That's great news. Thanks for calling. I'll let Cara know."

Her dad appeared in the kitchen doorway. "They picked up Brandt in the next county. He got into a fight with someone, pulled a gun, and a witness called the police. When they found out there was a warrant out on him, they arrested him."

Relief washed over Cara, and she exhaled deeply. It felt like she had been holding her breath ever since she received the note. Now she could breathe again.

Her dad crossed the room and hugged her close. "I'm glad that's over."

"Me too." She fist-pumped the air. "I can go back to my own house tomorrow."

Her mother clasped her hands. "We can celebrate Christmas in peace now."

Chapter 19

Friday, December 16

Josh showed up at the office on Friday to take Cara to lunch. She hadn't seen him since their lunch on Tuesday with Greg and Haley. He had been busy providing entertainment for holiday parties and luncheons. Word of his musical talent was spreading in Redwood. They had texted back and forth, but it wasn't the same as seeing him in person. She never ceased to be amazed how much she enjoyed his company after the way they had met and how much she had detested him in the beginning.

They stepped inside Mary's Sandwich Shop and grabbed the first empty table they came to.

Josh grinned as he pulled out her chair. "Guess what, the video has been taken down,"

"You're kidding." With all the chaos surrounding Brandt's return to Redwood, Cara had forgotten about the video. "What do you suppose happened?"

"Maybe our decision to ignore him worked. All I know is it wasn't there this morning when I checked."

"Let's hope it stays away." She glanced at the menu printed on the blackboard hanging on the wall behind the counter. "I think I'll have that strawberry pecan salad."

"Not me. I'm starved. I'm having the chicken fried steak."

When the waitress left with their order, Josh leaned across the table and lowered his voice. "How would you like to accompany me to a party at Emily Patterson's house tomorrow night?"

"Are you sure it's okay if I come along?"

Josh nodded. "Emily told me I could bring a date if I wanted to." He smiled. "You'll have to entertain yourself part of the time because I'm providing the music for the evening."

"That's okay. It will be fun. I like Emily and her fiancé Mark."

"Great. Paul and Carol are going also, so we can all ride together."

***

On Saturday night, Cara stood before her full-length mirror surveying her appearance wondering if Josh would like the black dress she had chosen. The lacey, white shawl she had purchased would add just the right touch. She smiled at herself, amazed that she was going out with him and cared what he thought. That day before Thanksgiving in the Grab it 'N Go seemed like a long time ago when in fact it had been less than a month.

The doorbell rang and she hurried to open it, picking up the shawl as she left the bedroom. She pulled open the door and froze. Brandt smiled back at her from the porch.

"I see you're ready for our date."

Fear paralyzed her and she struggled to speak. "What…are…you?"

"What's wrong, Cara? Surprised to see me?"

"I thought …"

"…I was in jail?" He waved his hand in dismissal. "I posted bail, my sweet."

Cara's body trembled as she stared at him. She glanced at the street. Where's Josh and Paul?

"Looking for someone?" Brandt asked, a grin twisting his lips. "There's no one here but me." He reached for the door.

Without a second thought, she slammed the door and turned the deadbolt. Where was her cell? The kitchen counter. She raced to get it. She could hear Brandt beating on the door.

"Cara, open the door."

She keyed in 9-1-1 with trembling fingers.

"Please help me. Someone is trying to break into my house. Tell Sheriff Willis it's Brandt Peters."

The sound of breaking glass reached her ears, and she clapped her hand over her mouth to keep from screaming.

Turn out the light. Go out the back door.

She didn't question the voice in her mind. She hurried to the door, flipped the light switch, and slipped outside. Without another thought, she raced to the neighbor's house and pounded on their back door.

Karen Potts opened the door. "Hi Cara." Her expression turned worried. "What's wrong? Why are you coming to the back?"

"Please …" she gasped, "let me in." She forced her way between Karen and the door. "Brandt is at my house … threatening me."

Karen immediately shut and locked the door then reached for Cara's arm. "Are you alright? Did you call 9-1-1?"

Cara nodded, trying to gain control of her heaving breaths.

Karen led her into the den where her husband watched TV. He looked up in surprise when he saw Cara. "Hey, Cara." He frowned. "What's wrong?"

"Brandt is next door trying to break into Cara's house." Karen grabbed her hand and squeezed it.

George stood, walked to the window, and looked out. "Someone just pulled up in front of your house."

Cara rushed to the window. Josh stepped out of the rental car Paul was driving. "Oh, no, it's Josh. Brandt will hurt him."

She started for the front door, but George grabbed her arm. "You can't go out there. I'll go."

Cara and Karen watched from the

window as George approached Brandt from the side. They heard George speak to him.

"Brandt, can I help you?"

Brandt's head jerked around at the sound of George's voice. "I don't need your help. I'm here to see Cara." He pivoted to see Josh and Paul approaching from the rear. He reached inside his coat and pulled out a gun. The three men stopped.

Cara gasped. "Oh, dear God, no. Please don't let him hurt anyone." She went to the front door and stepped out on the porch. Karen walked up behind her and grabbed her arm.

"Don't say anything," Karen whispered into her ear. "It might set him off."

Brandt waved the gun back and forth. "Why are you people sticking your nose in my business? This doesn't concern you."

"If it concerns Cara, it concerns me." Josh's voice carried across the two yards.

Brandt whirled in his direction and pointed the gun at him. "You stay away from her. She belongs to me."

Cara's heart thudded against her chest, and she gripped Karen's hand.

"Maybe we should ask her about that," Josh replied.

George inched closer to Brandt.

Josh kept talking. "Knock on the door and we'll ask her."

Something caught Cara's attention down the street. A figure approached quietly. Another one came from behind Cara's house while a third crouching figure crossed the street in front of Karen and George's house.

"Well, what's it gonna be, Peters?" Josh took a step forward.

"Shut up or I'll close your mouth for you," Brandt waved the gun at him.

Without warning, George launched himself at Brandt and they went sprawling across Cara's yard. The gun skittered across the lawn. Brandt yelled and fought but George's weight kept him pinned to the ground. Josh and Paul moved forward to assist George just as the three figures ran toward the porch. It was then she noticed their uniforms. Sheriff Willis helped George to his feet while the two deputies took charge of Brandt.

Josh hurried toward the front door of Cara's house.

"Josh, I'm over here."

He turned at her voice and then ran toward her. She met him at the bottom of the steps and flew into his arms. She buried her face in his shoulder. He hugged her tight.

"It's okay. You're safe now. They've got him."

A patrol car came down the street. The two officers escorted Brandt across the yard. He spewed nonsense about his rights being violated all the way to the car.

Sheriff Willis walked across the yard. "We got him, Cara, thanks to your call. I need to ask you a few questions though."

She turned to Josh. "You better go on to Emily's without me."

Josh shook his head. "No way."

"Yes, way." She laid her hand against his cheek. "You promised to be there. I'll be fine now."

He pulled her closer. "I hate to leave you after what just happened."

"Cara, are you okay?"

She turned at the sound of her father's voice as he ran toward her. "Where did you come from?" She stepped away from Josh and hugged her dad.

"Ed called me when he got the dispatch about Brandt being here."

"I'm fine, Dad." She looked back at Josh. "I had lots of help."

Her dad turned to Josh and extended his hand. "Thank you."

Josh shrugged. "I didn't do a whole lot."

Sheriff Willis slapped him on the back. "Don't discount the fact that you kept Peters talking while we made our way to him." He turned to George who now stood next to Karen. "You took a big chance, Sir. Thanks for your help."

George nodded. "Anytime."

Cara turned back to Josh. "Go to the party and play for them. You can call me when you head home."

Josh frowned. "Are you sure? I think Ms. Patterson would forgive me if she knew what happened here tonight."

Don Phillips slipped his arm around Cara. "Go ahead, Josh. I'll stay with Cara."

Josh let out his breath in a rush. "Okay." He reached out and touched Cara's arm. "I'll call as soon as I get back." He looked at her for a moment then hurried to the car where Paul and Carol waited for him.

Her dad hugged Cara close. "Seems to me that young man cares for you a great deal."

She nodded. "I think you're right, Dad."

Chapter 20

Sunday, Christmas Day

Cara pulled into the parking space at the church and glanced in the visor mirror to check her hair and lipstick. She wanted to look nice for Josh today. Since the incident with Brandt, her job had kept her busy during the day and he was scheduled every night and some days to play concerts for community holiday activities and private parties. His name had become well-known and in high demand in a short period of time. He had even been invited to play at a couple of places in neighboring towns. A lot of texts had flown back and forth between them, but today they would spend together, celebrating and worshipping with both families.

Someone tapped on the window, and Cara looked up to see Josh's smiling face peering at her.

She opened the door and climbed out. He pulled her into a hug.

"Josh. What will people think?"

"They'll think that I'm glad to see my girl." He grinned at her. "And they would be right." He squeezed her. "I've missed you."

"I've missed you too."

"Hope I'm not interrupting."

They both turned at the sound of a man's voice. He stood a few feet away.

Cara felt Josh's body tense next to her.

"Adam, what brings you to Redwood today?" Josh's voice took on a stern tone.

Adam looked at the ground and then back at Josh. "I came to apologize for the video and for the way I acted the last time we saw each other." He turned and looked at the church. "I thought I might go inside today."

Josh raised an eyebrow. "You? In a church?"

Adam nodded. "You're responsible you know. I could see a big change in you the last time we talked. There has to be something special about this church to make that kind of change in you."

Josh walked over to Adam and clasped his shoulder. "It's not the church that changed me, Adam. It's the one whose birth we're celebrating today. And you're welcome to come inside." He turned to Cara. "This is Adam."

Adam glanced over at Cara. "I guess I owe you a big apology for what happened. I never meant for you to be a part of it."

Cara smiled. "Apology accepted." She stepped over to Josh's side and slipped her arm through his. "Besides, I might not have met Josh otherwise."

Josh chuckled. "Come on. We need to get inside."

The three of them parted ways once inside the building. Josh took his place with the orchestra, Cara went to sit with her parents, and Adam found an empty seat near the back.

The choir opened with "The Hallelujah Chorus" from Handel's "Messiah" and Cara listened to the words for the first time in many years. A warmth settled over her as the music progressed.

She glanced at Josh and saw a glow about him she had never noticed before. There had been a big change in him. He wasn't the same man who had held a plastic gun on her in Ralph's Grab It 'N Go. Last Christmas, she wouldn't have believed she could feel something special for a man again.

When the song ended, Paul came to the front, but before he could say anything, a man approached him. Cara gasped. Adam stepped up to Paul and whispered something to him.

Paul nodded and turned to the congregation. "This is Adam, and he has something to share this morning."

Adam turned to face the crowd. His hands shook. A noticeable silence settled over the congregation.

Adam swallowed hard. "You don't know me, but I owe this church a big apology." A tear trickled down his cheek. "I'm the one who spray painted your nativity a couple of weeks ago." He took a deep breath and let it out slowly. "I'm so sorry." Tears rolled down both cheeks. "I've done a lot of things in my life, but this one I regret more than any of the other things I've done." He took a deep breath again and swiped at his face. "I hope you can forgive me." He turned and started across the platform. Josh stood from his spot and started walking toward

Adam. He intercepted him in the center and embraced him.

Beside her, Cara's dad stood to his feet and began to applaud. She stood with him and then people stood all over the building, the clapping bouncing off the walls of the church. The two men on the platform released each other and went back to their seats.

Paul took his place at the front again. "What we have witnessed this morning is the true spirit of Christmas. We have seen repentance, forgiveness, and love in action. Isn't that why Christ came over 2000 years ago as a baby? To bring those very things to us on earth?"

Cara bowed her head.

Forgive me for doubting you. I was wrong. This is the real meaning of Christmas. From now on, I celebrate your birth on this day.

Cara felt wetness on her own face, but she didn't wipe it away. Josh had called her friendship a gift and although she considered it unlikely when they first met, it had turned out to be special. But she had received another gift this Christmas also—a gift of grace. She didn't deserve it. She would call herself an unlikely candidate for that gift, except that the one who had given it considered her worth it and had come to earth to prove it to her.

When the service ended, Cara waited for Josh to reach her, then they walked out together. Adam stood next to a new nativity that had been set up on the church lawn. They walked over to him.

Adam extended his hand to Josh. "Thank you for being my friend. When I saw the change in you, I knew it was for real and I needed to do the same."

Josh grabbed his shoulder and squeezed it. "I'm glad it worked out for both of us."

Adam grinned. "My work here is done. I'm on my way to Dallas to spend some time with my family."

They watched him drive away then walked to Cara's car. She handed him the keys.

He held the door for her then went around to the driver's side and slid in.

Josh reached for her hand. "Merry Christmas, Cara."

"Merry Christmas to you, too."

He grinned. "This is my best Christmas ever."

She raised an eyebrow at him. "Why is that?"

"Out of all the gifts I've received through the years, you're the most unlikely gift I've ever gotten."

She squeezed his hand. "And it's the most unlikely gift I've ever given."

About the Author

Vickie Phelps writes to encourage, inspire, and influence. She is the author of eight novels and eight nonfiction books, three of which are coauthored with other writers. She has also published 200 articles, devotionals, and essays in more than fifty magazines and contributed to several anthologies. You can learn more at www.vickiephelps.com and connect with her on social media.

Facebook:
www.facebook.com/VickieSPhelps

Twitter:
www.twitter.com/VickieSPhelps

Pinterest: www.pinterest.com/vicphel

LinkedIn:
www.linkedin.com/in/VickieSPhelps

Instagram:
www.instagram.com/vphe1950

Amazon Author Page:

Amazon.com/author/vickiephelps

BOOKS BY VICKIE PHELPS

Fiction

The Redwood Series

Postmark From the Past

Wheels of Justice

If I Had it to Do Over

Moved, Left No Address

Waiting for Joy

A Christmas Legacy

The Cowboy's Christmas Star

Forgive the Trespassers

An Unlikely Gift

Nonfiction

Psalms for the Common Man

Gratitude: The Art of Being Thankful

10 Things to Remember When Times are Bad

The 5-Minute Prayer Plan for Women

The 5-Minute Prayer Plan for Moms

Co-authored with Jo Huddleston

Simply Christmas: Memories, Traditions &
Stories of the Season

Writing 101: A Handbook of Tips and
Encouragement for Writers

Co-authored with Emily Biggers

Mornings With God: My Daily Prayer
Journal

Note from the Author

Thank you for reading "An Unlikely Gift." I hope you enjoyed Cara's and Josh's story. If you did, would you take a minute and leave a review at Amazon, Goodreads, or one of the social media pages. Reviews are very important to authors, and we appreciate your support.

Thank you,
Vickie Phelps

Postmark From the Past

The Redwood Series, Book 1

Chapter 1

There was something strange about the faded, red envelope in her mailbox. Emily Patterson reached in and gingerly lifted it from the stack of mail. The edges appeared frayed and soiled, but the grimy appearance wasn't the only thing different.

No return address. No postage.

In spite of the icy wind slicing through every stitch she wore, Emily stood glued to the curb in front of her house, staring at what appeared to be her first holiday greeting of the season. Only when a passing car honked, shaking her out of her curious daze, did she realize she was freezing. She grabbed the rest of the mail and hurried up the walk.

Emily's numb fingers wrestled with the door key of the stately Victorian she'd called home for the past twenty years. Her grandfather, Sterling Patterson, who made his money in cattle, built the house in 1903. The house, something of an anomaly in the Panhandle, had been his way of proclaiming his status in the community of Redwood. The only Victorian in four counties, it sat just two blocks from the town square.

When she heard the familiar click of the lock, she breathed a frosty sigh of relief and let herself in. It was cold inside too, but nothing like the outside. After her grandparents passed away, her parents moved into the house. They renovated and updated with modern appliances, new velvet drapes, Persian rugs, and some of the finest artwork available. The one thing they didn't do was install a central heating system.

Every fall, Emily promised herself she would install heat before winter arrived. Now here it was, the twenty-seventh of November, and once again, she had let another year pass without doing so. But this evening something besides central heating occupied her mind. She tossed the rest of the mail on the hall table as she passed but carried the red envelope into the kitchen. She slid her fingernail beneath the seal, which lifted without any pressure, the yellowed adhesive confirming the passing of time.

The outdated illustration on the front puzzled her. And it looked soiled, like it had been handled a lot or maybe carried around in someone's pocket for a while. When she opened the card, a sheet of paper floated to the floor. She ignored it for a moment as she stared at the unfamiliar name on the card. *Mark*. Finally, she bent down and retrieved the sheet of paper.

Dear Emily,

I hope you will forgive me for being such a coward. I never had the nerve to tell you how much I care about you. I wasn't sure how you felt about me, and I guess my pride wouldn't allow me to speak up for fear of being rejected. And then there's the matter of your parents. I'm sure they don't approve of me. But here I am, thousands of miles away, and I've decided it's now or never. When you stare death in the face every day like I do, your priorities change real fast. I don't know if I'll get out of this place alive, but if I do, I'm coming back for you. I have to go now. The sound of mortar fire is getting closer. Looks like we're in for it again Merry Christmas, Emily.

Love, Mark

Emily wrinkled her brow in confusion. Love? And he says he's coming back for me? Her heart gave a tiny leap. It had been a long time since a man had shown any interest in her. But then, not too many eligible bachelors resided in Redwood. She could count them on her fingers, and all of them were as old as Methuselah. Most of the men her age had families. All her old classmates had moved away or married someone else. Including Frank Butler.

She sighed at the thought of Frank. She'd passed up her one and only chance for marriage when she turned down his proposal twelve years ago. They'd dated off and on for five years after she finished college. Everyone expected them to get married, even Frank, but she just didn't have the courage to marry someone she didn't love. Being fond of a man didn't qualify him as a lifelong companion. Or did it? Could she have been any lonelier than she was now if she had married Frank? He'd said he would wait until she was ready, but he didn't.

Frank had married and raised a family with someone else. He always tipped his Stetson when they happened into each other, but he never spoke. At first, she'd been offended by this formal gesture, but then she realized he'd given her every opportunity to accept his proposal. He'd been hurt and probably a little humiliated when she continued to put him off month after month.

She glanced down at the letter again. Mortar fire? Thousands of miles away? He must be in a foreign country. She turned the card over. Tiny brown spots dotted the back like something had splattered on it.

Emily reread the letter, hoping to find a missing clue, but there was nothing to enlighten her as to its author. This was just someone's idea of a bad joke. She tossed the card on the kitchen table and rubbed her freezing hands together. Thank goodness Clifford had been kind enough to stack some wood inside the porch for her last week. If it weren't for good neighbors like Cliff, she'd be in serious trouble.

Minutes later, with the fireplace blazing, Emily went back to the kitchen, grateful she had made a pot of beef stew over the weekend. She needed a steaming bowl of food to fight off the bone-numbing cold whistling around the corner of the house. She carried her meal to the living room and ate in front of the fireplace, still puzzling about the strange Christmas card. When the fire died down to a few glowing embers and the room grew chilly again, she turned out the light and headed for the bedroom.

It was only after she put on her blue flannel pajamas and slid beneath the quilts that she remembered what the letter said about her parents not approving. Her parents were dead, and she was an adult, so what did it matter? Something's wrong here. She threw back the covers, slipped on her house shoes, and made her way to the kitchen. The red envelope lay upside down where she had discarded it. She turned it over and squinted at the faded postmark. December 1, 1968.

Someone mailed me a Christmas card in 1968, and I'm just now receiving it in 1989? A chill crept up her spine, and goose bumps formed on her arms.

Had she known a Mark somebody back then? She was only eighteen, a senior in high school. But how could she forget someone in

Redwood?

Emily walked over to the bookshelf and pulled out her 1968 high school yearbook. She blew the dust off and carried it to the sofa. For the next few minutes, she searched through every roster, looking for anyone named Mark. She browsed through the senior class of which she'd been a part. With that shoulder-length style from the sixties, her own portrait didn't resemble the woman she was today. She leaned back and closed her eyes, willing herself to remember 1968.

Let's see. High school graduation. And those terrible riots. Robert Kennedy and Martin Luther King were assassinated. All the boys started shipping out to Vietnam.

Emily chewed on her lip for a moment, conjuring up images of the past.

What a horrible time, all those boys getting killed; their mangled bodies shipped home to their families. Lenny Burnett never made it home. They never found him. His mother died of a broken heart.

Emily opened her eyes and sat up. Mark must have been in Vietnam when he wrote the letter. That would explain the mortar fire. But it still didn't tell her who he is, or why she was just now receiving it.

Closing the yearbook, she yawned and climbed back in bed. Emily closed her eyes, but all she could think about was the mysterious

Mark from 1968. What had happened to him? Why didn't he ever come to see her? A chilling thought crossed her mind. Maybe he didn't make it home alive. Or maybe he was an MIA or POW.

Emily opened her eyes and rolled onto her side. She had to quit thinking about him. A faint light streamed through the open shade on her window. In the glow from the streetlamp on the corner, she could see the first snowflakes beginning to fall. The snow reminded her of the fragrant white talcum powder her mother used to sprinkle on after her bath. The snow, like the powder, clung to whatever surface it landed upon. Sadness swept over Emily. She still missed her parents, especially at Christmastime. The wintry scene outside her window blurred as tears stung her eyes.

Dear God, I can't stand to spend another Christmas alone.